THE HIDDE

&

Other Stories

THE HIDDEN TREASURE

&
Other Stories

Rabindranath Tagore

Rupa & Co

Concept and typeset Copyright © Rupa & Co 2007

Published 2007 by
Rupa . Co
7/16, Ansari Road, Daryaganj,
New Delhi 110 002

Sales Centres:

Allahabad Bangalore Chandigarh Chennai
Hyderabad Jaipur Kathmandu
Kolkata Mumbai Pune

Typeset in
Nikita Overseas Pvt Ltd,
19A Ansari Road,
New Delhi 110 002

Printed in India by
Gopsons Papers Ltd
A-14, Sector 60
Noida 201 301

Contents

Contents

The Hidden Treasure

It was a moonless night, and Mrityunjaya was seated before the ancestral image of the goddess Kali. As he finished his devotions the cawing of an early morning crow was heard from a neighbouring mango grove.

First seeing that the door of the temple was shut, he bowed once more before the image and, shifting its pedestal, took from under it a strong wooden box. This he opened with a key which hung on his sacred thread, but the moment he had looked inside he started in dismay. He took up the box and shook it several times. It had not been broken open, for the lock was uninjured. He groped all round the image a dozen times, but could find nothing.

Mrityunjaya's little temple stood on one side of his inner garden which was surrounded by a wall. It was sheltered by the shade of some tall trees. Inside there was nothing but the image of Kali, and it had only one entrance. Like a mad man Mrityunjaya threw open the door, and began to roam round on all sides in search of a clue, but in vain. By this time daylight had come. In despair he sat on some steps and with his head buried in his hands began to think. He was just beginning to feel sleepy after his long sleepless night when suddenly he heard someone say: "Greeting, my son!" Looking up he saw in the courtyard before him a long-haired sannyasi. Mrityunjaya made a deep obeisance to him and the ascetic placed his hand on his head, saying: "My son, your sorrow is vain."

Mrityunjaya, in astonishment, replied: "Can you read people's thoughts? How do you know about my sorrow? I have spoken of it to no one."

The sannyasi answered: "My son, instead of sorrowing over what you have lost, you ought to rejoice."

Clasping his feet Mrityunjaya exclaimed: "Then you know everything? Tell me how it got lost and where I can recover it."

The sannyasi replied: "If I wanted you to suffer misfortune then I would tell you. But you must not grieve over that which the goddess has taken from you out of pity."

But Mrityunjaya was not satisfied and in the hope of pleasing his visitor he spent the whole of that day serving him in different ways. But when early next morning he was bringing him a bowl of fresh milk from his own cow he found that the sannyasi had disappeared.

2

When Mrityunjaya had been a child his grandfather, Harihar, was sitting one day on those same steps of the temple, smoking his *hookah,* when a sannyasi came into the courtyard and greeted him. Harihar invited him into his home and for several days treated him as an honoured guest.

When about to go the sannyasi said to him: "My son, you are poor, are you not?", to which Harihar replied: "Father, I am indeed. Only hear what my condition is. Once our family was the most prosperous in the village but now our condition is so miserable that we can hardly hold up our heads. I beg you to tell me how we can restore ourselves to prosperity again."

The sannyasi laughing slightly said: "My son, why not be satisfied with your present position? What's the use of trying to become wealthy?"

But Harihar persisted and declared that he was ready to undertake anything that would restore his family to their proper rank in society.

Thereupon the sannyasi took out a roll of cloth in which an old and stained piece of paper was wrapped. It looked like a horoscope. The sannyasi unrolled it and Harihar saw that it had some signs in cypher written within circles, and below these was a lot of doggerel verse which commenced thus:

> *For attainment of your goal*
> *Find a word that rhymes with soul.*
> *From the 'rādhā' take its 'dhā',*
> *After that at last put 'rā'.*
> *From the tamarind-banyan's mouth*
> *Turn your face towards the south.*
> *When the light is in the East*
> *There shall be of wealth a feast.*

There was much more of the same kind of rigmarole.

Harihar said: "Father, I can't understand a single word of it."

To this the sannyasi replied: "Keep it by you. Make your *puja* to the goddess Kali and by her grace you, or some descendant of yours, will gain the untold wealth of which this writing tells the secret hiding place."

Harihar entreated him to explain the writing, but the sannyasi said that only by the practice of austerity could its meaning be discovered.

Just at this moment Harihar's youngest brother, Shankar, arrived on the scene and Harihar tried to snatch the paper away before it could be observed. But the sannyasi, laughing, said: "Already, I see, you have started on the painful road to greatness. But you need not be afraid. The secret can only be discovered by one person. If anyone else tries a thousand times he will never be able to solve it. It will be a member of your family, so you can show this paper to anyone without fear."

The sannyasi having left them, Harihar could not rest until he had hidden the paper. Fearful lest anyone else should profit by it, and above all lest his young brother Shankar should enjoy this hidden wealth, he locked the paper in a strong wooden box and hid it under the seat of the household goddess Kali. Every month, at the time of the new moon, he would go in the dead of night to the temple and there he would offer prayers to the goddess in the hope that she would give him the power to decipher the secret writing.

Some time after this Shankar came to his brother and begged him to show him the paper.

"Go away, you idiot!" shouted Harihar, "that paper was nothing. That rascal of a sannyasi wrote a lot of nonsense on it simply to deceive me. I burnt it long ago."

Shankar remained silent, but some weeks afterwards he disappeared from the house and was never seen again.

From that time Harihar gave up all other occupations, and spent all his waking moments in thinking about the hidden treasure.

When he died he left this mysterious paper to his eldest son, Shyamapada, who, as soon as he got possession of it, gave up his business and spent his whole time in studying the secret cypher and in worshipping the goddess in the hope of goodluck coming to him.

Mrityunjaya was Shyamapada's eldest child, so he became the owner of this precious heirloom on his father's death. The worse his condition became the greater the eagerness he showed in trying to solve the secret. It was about this time that the loss of the paper occurred. The visit of the long-haired sannyasi coinciding with its disappearance, Mrityunjaya determined that he would try to find him, feeling sure he could discover everything from him. So he left his home on the quest.

3

After spending a year in going from place to place Mrityunjaya one day arrived at a village named Dharagole. There he stayed at a grocer's shop, and as he was sitting absent-mindedly smoking and thinking, a sannyasi passed along the edge of a neighbouring field. At first Mrityunjaya did not pay much attention, but after a few minutes he came to himself and it flashed across his mind that that was the very sannyasi for whom he had been searching. Hurriedly laying aside his *hookah* he rushed past the startled storekeeper and dashed from the shop into the street. But the sannyasi was nowhere to be seen.

As it was dark and the place was strange to him he gave up the idea of searching further and returned to the shop. There he asked the storekeeper what lay beyond the village in the great forest near by. The man replied:

"Once a great city was there, but owing to the curse of the sage Agastya, its king and all his subjects died of some dreadful pestilence. People say that enormous wealth and piles of jewels are still hidden there, but no one dares to enter that forest even at midday. Those who have done so have never returned."

Mrityunjaya's mind became restless, and all night long he lay on his mat tormented by mosquitoes and by thoughts of the forest, the sannyasi, and his lost secret. He had read the verses so often that he could almost repeat them by heart, and hour after hour the opening lines kept ringing through his mind, until his brain reeled:

> *For attainment of your goal*
> *Find a word that rhymes with soul.*
> *From the 'rādhā' take its 'dhā'*
> *After that at last put 'rā'.*

He could not get the words out of his head. At last when dawn came he fell asleep and in a dream the meaning of the verse became as clear as day-light. Taking the 'dhā' from 'rādhā' and at the end of that putting 'rā' you get 'dhārā', and 'gole' rhymes with soul! The name of the village in which he was staying was 'Dhārāgole'! He jumped up from his mat sure that he was at last near the end of his search.

4

The whole of that day Mrityunjaya spent roaming about the forest in the hope of finding a path. He returned to the village at night half dead with hunger and fatigue, but next day he took a bundle of parched rice and started off again. At midday he arrived at the side of a lake round which there were traces of a path. The water was clear in the middle but near the banks it was a tangle of weeds and water-lilies. Having soaked his rice in the water by some broken stone steps on the bank he finished eating it and began to walk slowly round the lake looking carefully everywhere for signs of buildings. Suddenly when he had reached the west side of the lake he stood stock still, for there before him was a tamarind tree growing right in the centre of a gigantic banyan. He immediately recalled the lines:

From the tamarind-banyan's mouth
Turn your face towards the south.

After walking some distance towards the south he found himself in the middle of a thick jungle through which it was impossible to force a way. He however determined not to lose sight of the tamarind tree.

Turning back he noticed in the distance through the branches of the tree the pinnacles of a building.

Making his way in that direction he came upon a ruined temple, by the side of which were the ashes of a recent fire. With great caution Mrityunjaya made his way to a broken door and peeped in. There was no one there, not even an image, only a blanket, and a water pot with a sannyasi's scarf lying beside it.

Evening was approaching, the village was far off, and it would be difficult to find a path back by night, so Mrityunjaya was pleased at seeing signs of a human being. By the door lay a large piece of stone which had fallen from the ruin. On this he seated himself and was deep in thought when he suddenly noticed what appeared to be written characters on the surface of the stone. Looking closely he saw a circular symbol which was familiar to him. It was partly obliterated, it is true, but it was sufficiently distinct for him to recognize the design as that which had appeared at the top of his lost piece of paper. He had studied it so often that it was clearly printed on his brain. How many times had he begged the goddess to reveal to him the meaning of that mystic sign as he sat at midnight in the dimly lit temple of his home with the fragrance of incense filling the night air. Tonight the fulfilment of his long cherished desire seemed so near that his whole body trembled. Fearing that by some slight blunder he might frustrate all his hopes, and above all dreading lest the sannyasi had been beforehand in discovering his treasure he shook with terror. He could not decide what to do. The thought came to him that he might even at that very moment be sitting above untold wealth without knowing it.

As he sat repeating the name of Kali, evening fell and the sombre darkness of the forest resounded with the continual chirping of crickets.

5

Just as he was wondering what to do he saw through the thick foliage the distant gleam of a fire. Getting up from the stone on which he was seated he carefully marked the spot he was leaving and went off in the direction of the light.

Having progressed with great difficulty a short way he saw from behind the trunk of a tree the very sannyasi he had been seeking with the well-known paper in his hand. He had opened it and, by the light of the flames, he was working out its meaning in the ashes with a stick.

There was the very paper which belonged to Mrityunjaya and which had belonged to his father and his grandfather before him, in the hands of a thief and a cheat! It was for this then that this rogue of a sannyasi had bidden Mrityunjaya not to sorrow over his loss!

The sannyasi was calculating the meaning of the signs, and every now and then would measure certain distances on the ground with a stick. Sometimes he would stop and shake his head with a disappointed air, and then he would go back and make fresh calculations.

In this way the night was nearly spent and it was not until the cool breeze of daybreak began to rustle in the leafy branches of the trees that the sannyasi folded up the paper and went away.

Mrityunjaya was perplexed. He was quite sure that without the sannyasi's help it would be impossible for him to decipher the mystery of the paper. But he was equally certain that the covetous rascal would not knowingly assist him. Therefore to watch the sannyasi secretly was his only hope; but as he could not get any food without going back to the village, Mrityunjaya decided he would return to his lodgings that morning.

When it became light enough he left the tree behind which he had been hiding and made his way to the place where the sannyasi had been making his calculations in the ashes. But he could make nothing of the marks. Nor, after wandering all round, could he see that the forest there differed in any way from other parts of the jungle.

As the sunlight began to penetrate the thick shade of the trees Mrityunjaya made his way towards the village, looking carefully on every side as he went. His chief fear was lest the sannyasi should catch sight of him.

That morning a feast was given to Brahmins at the shop where Mrityunjaya had taken shelter, so he came in for a sumptuous meal. Having fasted so long he could not resist eating heavily, and after the feast he soon rolled over on his mat and fell sound asleep.

Although he had not slept all night, Mrityunjaya had made up his mind that he would that day take his meals in good time and start off early in the afternoon. What happened was exactly the opposite, for when he woke the sun had already set. But although it was getting dark, he could not refrain from entering the forest.

Night fell suddenly and so dense was the darkness that it was impossible for him to see his way through the deep shadows of the thick jungle. He could not make out which way he was going and when day broke he found that he had been going round and round in one part of the forest quite near the village.

The raucous cawing of some crows from near by sounded to Mrityunjaya like mockery.

After many miscalculations and corrections the sannyasi had at length discovered the path to the entrance of a subterranean tunnel. Lighting a torch he entered. The brick walls were mouldy with moss and slime, and water oozed out from the many cracks. In some places sleeping toads could be seen piled up in heaps. After proceeding over slippery stones for some distance the sannyasi came to a wall. The passage was blocked! He struck the wall in several places with a heavy iron bar but there was not the least suspicion of a hollow sound. There was not a crack anywhere; without a doubt the tunnel ended there.

He spent the whole of that night studying the paper again, and next morning having finished his calculations, he entered the underground passage once more. This time, carefully following the secret directions, he loosened a stone from a certain place and discovered a branch turning. This he followed, but once more he came to a stop where another wall blocked all further progress.

But finally, on the fifth night, the sannyasi as he entered exclaimed: "Tonight I shall find the way without the shadow of a doubt!"

The passage was like a labyrinth. There seemed no end to its branches and turnings. In some places it was so low and narrow that he had to crawl on hands and knees. Carefully holding the torch he arrived at length at a large circular room, in the middle of which was a wide well of solid masonry. By the light of his torch the sannyasi was unable to see how deep it was, but he saw that from the roof there descended into it a thick heavy iron chain. He pulled with all his strength at this chain and it shook very slightly. But there rose from the depth of the well a metallic clang which reverberated through that dark dismal chamber. The sannyasi called out in excitement: "At last I have found it!"

Next moment a huge stone rolled through the hole in the broken wall through which he had entered and someone fell on the floor with a loud cry. Startled by this sudden sound the sannyasi let his torch fall to the ground and the room was plunged in darkness.

7

He called out "Who is there?" but there was no answer. Putting out his hand he touched a man's body. Shaking it. he asked, "Who are you?" Still he got no reply. The man was unconscious.

Striking a flint he at last found his torch and lighted it. In the meantime the man had regained consciousness and was trying to sit up though he was groaning with pain.

On seeing him the sannyasi exclaimed: "Why, it is Mrityunjaya! What are you doing here?"

Mrityunjaya replied: "Father, pardon me. God has punished me enough. I was trying to roll that stone on you when my foot slipped and I fell. My leg must be broken."

To this the sannyasi answered: "But what good would it have done you to kill me?"

Mrityunjaya exclaimed: "What good indeed! Why did you steal into my temple and rob me of that secret paper? And what are you doing in this underground place yourself? You are a thief, and a cheat! The sannyasi who gave that paper to my grandfather told him that one of his family was to discover the secret of the writing. The secret is mine by rights and it is for this reason that I have been following you day and night like your shadow, going without food and sleep all these days. Then today when you exclaimed 'At last I have found it!' I could restrain myself no longer. I had followed you and was hiding behind the wall where you had made the hole, and I tried to kill you. I failed because I am weak and the ground was slippery and I fell. Kill me if you wish, then I can become a guardian spirit to watch over this treasure of mine. But if I live, you will never be able to take it. Never! Never! Never! If you try, I will bring the curse of a Brahmin on you by jumping into this well and committing suicide. Never will you be able to enjoy this treasure. My father, and his father before him, thought of nothing but this treasure and they died thinking of it. We have become poor for its sake. In search of it I have left wife and children, and without food or sleep have wandered from place to place like a maniac. Never shall you take this treasure from me while I have eyes to see!"

8

The sannyasi said quietly: "Mrityunjaya, listen to me. I will tell you everything. You remember that your grandfather's youngest brother was called Shankar?"

"Yes," replied Mrityunjaya, "he left home and was never heard of again."

"Well," said the sannyasi, "I am that Shankar!"

Mrityunjaya gave a gasp of despair. He had so long regarded himself as the sole owner of this hidden wealth that, now that this relative had turned up and proved his equal right, he felt as if his claim were destroyed.

Shankar continued: "From the moment that my brother got that paper from the sannyasi he tried every means in his power to keep it hidden from me. But the harder he tried the greater became my curiosity, and I soon found that he had hidden it in a wooden box under the seat of the goddess. I got hold of a duplicate key, and by degrees, whenever the opportunity occurred, I copied out the whole of the writing and the signs. The very day I had finished copying it I left home in quest of the treasure. I even left my wife and only child neither of whom is now living. There is no need to describe all the places I visited in my wanderings. I felt sure that as the paper had been given to my brother by a sannyasi I would be able to find out its meaning from one, so I began to serve sannyasis whenever I had the chance. Many of them were impostors and tried to steal the writing from me. In this way many years passed, but not for a single moment did I have any peace or happiness.

"At last in my search, by virtue of some right action in a previous birth, I had the good fortune to meet in the mountains Swami Rupananda. He said to me: 'My child, give up desire, and the imperishable wealth of the whole universe will be yours.'

"He cooled the fever of my mind. By his grace the light of the sky and the green verdure of the earth seemed to me equal to the wealth of kings. One winter day at the foot of the mountain I lit a fire in the brazier of my revered *Guru* and offered up the paper in its flames. The Swami laughed slightly as I did it. At the time I did not understand that laugh. But now I do. Doubtless he thought it is easy enough to burn a piece of paper, but to burn to ashes our desires is not so simple!

"When not a vestige of the paper remained it seemed as if my heart had suddenly filled with the rare joy of freedom. My mind at last realized the meaning of detachment. I said to myself, 'Now I have no more fear, I desire nothing in the world.'

"Shortly after this I parted from the Swami and although I have often sought for him since, I have never seen him again.

"I then wandered as a sannyasi with my mind detached from worldly things. Many years passed and I had almost forgotten the existence of the paper, when one day I came to the forest near Dharagole and took shelter in a ruined temple. After a day or two I noticed that there were inscriptions on the walls, some of which

I recognized. There could be no doubt that here was a clue to what I had spent so many years of my life in trying to discover. I said to myself: 'I must not stay here. I must leave this forest.'

"But I did not go. I thought there was no harm in staying to see what I could find out, just to satisfy my curiosity. I examined the signs carefully, but without result. I kept thinking of the paper I had burnt. Why had I destroyed it? What harm would there have been in keeping it?

"At last I went back to the village of my birth. On seeing the miserable condition of my ancestral home I thought to myself: 'I am a sannyasi, I have no need of wealth for myself, but these poor people have a home to keep up. There can be no sin in recovering the hidden treasure for their benefit.'

"I knew where the paper was, so it was not difficult for me to steal it.

"For a whole year since then I have been living in this lonely forest searching for the clue. I could think of nothing else. The oftener I was thwarted the greater did my eagerness become. I had the unflagging energy of a mad man as I sat night after night concentrating on the attempt to solve my problem.

"When it was that you discovered me I do not know. If I had been in an ordinary frame of mind you would never have remained concealed, but I was so absorbed in my task that I never noticed what was going on around me.

"It was not until today that I discovered at last what I had been so long searching for. The treasure hidden here is greater than that of the richest king in the world, and to find it the meaning of only one more sign had to be deciphered.

"This secret is the most difficult of all, but in my mind I had come even to its solution. That was why I cried out in my delight, 'At last I have found it!' If I wish I can in a moment enter that hidden storehouse of gold and jewels."

Mrityunjaya fell at Shankar's feet and exclaimed:

"You are a sannyasi, you have no use for wealth— but take me to that treasure. Do not cheat me again!"

Shankar replied: "Today the last link of my fetters is broken! That stone which you intended should kill me did not indeed strike my body but it has shattered forever the folly of my infatuation. Today I have seen how monstrous is the image of desire. That calm and incomprehensible smile of my saintly *Guru* has at last kindled the inextinguishable lamp of my soul."

Mrityunjaya again begged pitifully: "You are free, but I am not. I do not even want freedom. You must not cheat me of this wealth."

The sannyasi answered: "Very well, my son, take this paper of yours, and if you can find this treasure, keep it."

Saying this the sannyasi handed the paper and his staff to Mrityunjaya and left him alone. Mrityunjaya called out in despair: "Have pity on me. Do not leave me. Show me the treasure!" But there was no answer.

Mrityunjaya dragged himself up and with the help of the stick tried to find his way out of the tunnels, but they were such a maze that he was again and again completely puzzled. At last worn out he lay down and fell asleep.

When he awoke there was no means of telling whether it was night or day. As he felt hungry he ate some parched rice, and again began to grope for the way out. At length in despair he stopped and called out: "Oh! Sannyasi, where are you?" His cry echoed and re-echoed through the tangled labyrinth of those underground tunnels, and when the sound of his own voice had died away, he heard from close by a reply, "I am near you—what is it you want?"

Mrityunjaya answered: "Have pity on me and show me where the treasure is."

There was no answer, and although he called again and again all was silent.

After a time Mrityunjaya fell asleep again in this underground realm of perpetual darkness where there was neither night nor day. When he woke up and found it still dark he called out beseechingly: "Oh! Sannyasi, tell me where you are."

The answer came from near at hand: "I am here. What do you want?"

Mrityunjaya answered: "I want nothing now but that you should rescue me from this dungeon."

The sannyasi asked: "Don't you want the treasure?"

Mrityunjaya replied: "No."

There was the sound of a flint being struck and the next moment there was a light. The sannyasi said: "Well Mrityunjaya, let us go."

Mrityunjaya: "Then, father, is all my trouble to be in vain? Shall I never obtain that wealth?"

Immediately the torch went out. Mrityunjaya exclaimed "How cruel!', and sat down in the silence to think. There was no means of measuring time and the darkness was without end. How he wished that he could with all the strength of his mind and body shatter that gloom to atoms. His heart began to feel restless for the light, for the open sky, and for all the varied beauty of the world, and he called out: "Oh! Sannyasi, cruel sannyasi, I do not want the treasure. I want you to rescue me."

The answer came: "You no longer want the treasure? Then take my hand, and come with me."

This time no torch was lighted. Mrityunjaya holding his stick in one hand and clinging to the sannyasi with the other slowly began to move. After twisting and turning many times through the maze of tunnels they came to a place where the sannyasi said, "Now stand still."

Standing still Mrityunjaya heard the sound of an iron door opening. The next moment the sannyasi seized his hand, and said: "Come!"

Mrityunjaya advanced into what appeared to be a vast hall. He heard the sound of a flint being struck and then the blaze of the torch revealed to his astonished eyes the most amazing sight that he had ever dreamed of. On every side thick plates of gold were arranged in piles. They stood against the walls glittering like heaped rays of solid sunlight stored in the bowels of the earth. Mrityunjaya's eyes began to gleam. Like a mad man he cried: "All this gold is mine—I will never part with it!"

"Very well," replied the sannyasi, "here is my torch, some barley and parched rice, and this large pitcher of water for you. Farewell."

And as he spoke the sannyasi went out, clanging the heavy iron door behind him.

Mrityunjaya began to go round and round the hall touching the piles of gold again and again. Seizing some small pieces he threw them down on the floor, he lifted them into his lap, striking them one against another he made them ring, he even stroked his body all over with the precious metal. At length, tired out, he spread a large flat plate of gold on the floor, lay down on it, and fell asleep.

When he woke he saw the gold glittering on every side. There was nothing but gold. He began to wonder whether day had dawned and whether the birds were awake and revelling in the morning sunlight. It seemed as though in imagination he could smell the fragrant breeze of daybreak coming from the garden by the little lake near his home. It was as if he could actually see the ducks floating on the water, and hear their contented cackle as the maidservant came from the house to the steps of the ghat, with the brass vessels in her hand to be cleaned.

Striking the door Mrityunjaya called out: "Oh, Sannyasi, listen to me!"

The door opened and the sannyasi entered. "What do you want?" he asked.

"I want to go out," replied Mrityunjaya, "but can't I take away a little of this gold?"

Without giving any answer the sannyasi lighted a fresh torch, and placing a full water pot and a few handfuls of rice on the floor went out closing the door behind him.

Mrityunjaya took up a thin plate of gold, bent it and broke it into small fragments. These he scattered about the room like lumps of dirt. On some of them he made marks with his teeth. Then he threw a plate of gold on the floor and trampled on it. He asked himself, 'How many men in the world are rich enough to be able to throw gold about as I am doing!' Then he became oppressed with a fever for destruction. He was seized with a longing to crush all these heaps of gold into dust and sweep them away with a broom. In this way he could show his contempt for the covetous greed of all the kings and maharajahs in the world.

At last he became tired of throwing the gold about in this way and fell asleep. Again he saw on awakening those heaps of gold, and rushing to the door he struck at it with all his strength and called out: "Oh Sannyasi, I do not want this gold. I do not want it!"

But the door remained closed. Mrityunjaya shouted till his throat was hoarse and still the door did not open. He threw lump after lump of gold against it, but with no effect. He was in despair. Would the sannyasi leave him there to shrivel up and die, inch by inch, in that golden prison?

As Mrityunjaya watched the gold fear gripped him. Those piles of glittering metal surrounded him on all sides with a terrifying smile, hard, silent, without tremor or change, until his body began to tremble, his mind to quake. What connection had he with these heaps of gold? They could not share his feelings—they had no sympathy with him in his sorrows. They had no need of the light, or the sky. They did not long for the cool breezes, they did not even want life. They had no desire for freedom. In this eternal darkness they remained hard and bright for ever.

On earth perhaps sunset had come with its golden gift of limpid light—that golden light which cools the eyes as it bids farewell to the fading day, falling like tears on the face of darkness. Now the evening star would be gazing serenely down on the courtyard of his home where his young wife had tended the cows in the meadow and lit the lamp in the corner of the house, while the tinkling of the temple bell spoke of the closing ceremony of the day.

Today the most trifling events of his home and his village shone in Mrityunjaya's imagination with overpowering lustre. Even the thought of his old dog lying curled up asleep in front of the stove caused him pain. He thought of the grocer in whose shop he had stayed while he was at Dharagole and imagined him putting out his lamp, shutting up his shop and walking leisurely to some house in the village to take his evening meal, and as he thought of him he envied him his happiness. He did not know what day it was, but if it were Sunday he could picture to himself the villagers returning to their homes after market, calling their friends from over the fields and crossing the river together in the ferry boat. He could see a peasant, with a couple of fish dangling in his hand and a basket on his head, walking through the meadow paths, or making his way along the dikes of the paddy fields, past the bamboo fences of the little hamlets, returning to his village after the day's work in the dim light of the star-strewn sky.

The call came to him from the world of men. But layers of earth separated him from the most insignificant occurrences of life's varied and unceasing pilgrimage. That life, that sky, and that light appeared to him now as more priceless than all the treasures of the universe. He felt that if only he could for one moment again lie in the dusty lap of mother earth in her green clad beauty, beneath the free open spaces of the sky, filling his lungs with the fragrant breeze laden with the scents of mown grass and of blossoms, he could die feeling that his life was complete.

As these thoughts came to him the door opened, and the sannyasi entering asked: "Mrityunjaya, what do you want now?"

He answered: "I want nothing further. I want only to go out from this maze of darkness. I want to leave this delusive gold. I want light, and the sky; I want freedom!"

The sannyasi said: "There is another storehouse full of rarest gems of incalculable value, tenfold more precious than all this gold. Do you not wish to go there?"

Mrityunjaya answered: "No."

"Haven't you the curiosity just to see it once?"

"No, I don't want even to see it. If I have to beg in rags for the rest of my life I would not spend another moment here."

"Then come," said the sannyasi, and taking Mrityunjaya's hand he led him in front of the deep well. Stopping here he took out the paper and asked:

"And what will you do with this?"

Taking it Mrityunjaya tore it into fragments and threw them down the well.

Cloud and Sun

It had rained the previous day. But this morning there was no sign of rain and the pale sunlight and scattered clouds between them were painting the nearly-ripe autumnal corn-fields alternately with their long brushes; the broad green landscape was now being touched with light to a glittering whiteness, and again smeared over the next moment with the deep coolness of shadow.

While these two actors, sun and cloud, were playing their own parts by themselves with the whole sky for a stage, innumerable plays were being enacted down below in various places on the stage of the world.

In the particular place on which we are about to raise the curtain on one of life's little plays, a house can be seen by the side of a village lane. Only one of the outer rooms is brick-built, and on either side of it a dilapidated brick wall runs to encircle a few mud huts. From the lane one can discover through the grated window a young man with the upper half of his body uncovered, sitting on a plank bed, trying every now and then to drive away both heat and mosquitoes with a palm-leaf fan held in his left hand and reading attentively a book held in his right. Out in the village lane, a girl wearing a striped *sāri* with some black plums tied in a corner thereof, which she was engaged in demolishing one by one, kept passing again and again in front of the said grated window. From the expression of her face it could be clearly perceived that the young girl was on terms of intimacy with the person sitting and reading on the bed inside and that she was bent on attracting his attention somehow or other and letting him know by her silent contempt: 'Just now I am busily engaged in eating black plums and don't care a fig for you.'

Unfortunately, the man engaged in reading inside the room was short-sighted and the silent scorn of the girl could not touch him from afar. The girl herself knew this, so that after many fruitless journeyings to and fro, she was obliged to use pellets of plumstones in lieu of silent scorn. So difficult is it to preserve the purity of disdain when one has to deal with the blind.

When three or four stones thrown at random, as it were, every now and again rapped against the wooden door, the reader raised his head and looked out. When the designing young person came to know this, she began to choose succulent black plums from her *sāri*-knot with redoubled attention. The man, puckering his brows and straining his eyes, recognized the girl at last and putting down his book came up to the window and smilingly called out "Giribala!"

Giribala, while keeping her attention fixed steadily and wholly upon the task of examining the black plums tied in her *sāri-end*, proceeded to walk on slowly step by step.

Upon this it was brought home to the myopic young man that he was being punished for some unknown misdeed. Hurriedly coming outside he asked, "I say, how is it you haven't given me any plums today?" Turning a deaf ear to this question Giribala chose a plum after much searching and deliberation, and proceeded to eat it with the utmost composure.

These plums came from Giribala's home-garden, and were the daily prerequisite of the young man. But for some reason or other Giribala seemed to have forgotten this fact, and her behaviour went to indicate that she had gathered them for herself alone. However, it was not clear what the idea was of plucking fruit from one's own garden and coming and eating it ostentatiously in front of another's door. Hence the youth came out and caught hold of her hand. At first Giribala turned and twisted and tried to wriggle out of his grasp, but suddenly she burst into a flood of tears and scattering the plums from her *sāri* on to the ground, rushed away.

The restless sunlight and shadows of the morning had become tired and tranquil in the afternoon. White swollen clouds lay massed in a corner of the sky and the fading evening light glimmered upon the leaves of the trees, the water in the ponds, and every nook and corner of the rain-washed landscape. Again we see the girl in front of the grated window, and the young man sitting inside the room, the only difference being that there are no plums now in the girl's *sāri*-end, neither does the youth hold any book in his hand. There may have been certain other deeper and more serious differences also.

It is difficult to say what particular need had brought the girl again this afternoon to this particular spot. Whatever other grounds she may have had, it is quite apparent from her behaviour that talking to the man inside the room is not one of them. Rather it would appear as if she has come to see whether the plums she had scattered upon the ground this morning had sprouted in the afternoon.

But one of the principal reasons for their not sprouting was that the fruits were lying heaped up at present in front of the young man on the wooden bed; and whilst the girl was occupied in bending low every now and then in search of some imaginary object, the youth, suppressing his inward laughter, was gravely eating the plums one after another, after carefully selecting them. At length, when one or two stones came and fell by chance near the girl's feet or even upon them, she realized that the young man was paying her back for her fit of pique. But was this fair! When she had thrown overboard all the pride of her little heart and was seeking for some means of surrendering herself, wasn't it cruel of him to place an obstacle in her very difficult path? As the girl came to realize with a blush that she had been caught in the attempt of giving herself up, and began to seek some means of escape, the youth came out and caught hold of her hand.

This time too the girl turned and twisted and made several attempts to shake off his grasp and run away as she had done this morning; but she did not cry. On the other hand she flushed and, turning her head aside, hid her face on her tormentor's back and laughed profusely and, as if compelled by outward force alone, entered the iron-barred cell like a conquered captive.

Like the light play of sun and cloud in the sky, the play of these two human beings in a corner of the earth was equally trivial and equally transient. Again as the play of sun and cloud in the sky is not really unimportant and not really a game but only looks like it, so the humble history of an idle rainy day spent by these ordinary folk may seem to be of no account amidst the hundreds of events happening in this world; but as a matter of fact it was not so. The ancient and stupendous Fate that eternally weaves one age into another with unchanging sternness of countenance, that same Ancient was causing the seeds of grief and joy throughout the girl's whole life to sprout amidst the trivial tears and laughter of this morning and evening. And yet the uncalled-for grievance of the girl seemed altogether incomprehensible, not only to the onlookers, but also to the young man—the hero of this little play. Why the girl should get annoyed one day and lavish unbounded affection on another, why she should increase the rations one day and on another stop them altogether, was not easy to understand. Some day it was as if all her powers of imagination and thought and skill were concentrated on giving pleasure to the young man; again on another day she would muster all her limited stock of energy and hardness to try and hurt him. When she failed to wound him her hardness was redoubled; when she succeeded, it was dissolved in profuse showers of repentant tears and flowed in a thousand streams of affection.

The first part of the trivial history of this trivial play of sun and shadow is briefly narrated in the following chapter.

2

All the other people in the village were occupied with factions, plotting against one another, sugarcane planting, false lawsuits and trade in jute; the only ones interested in ideas and literature were Sashibhushan and Giribala.

There was no call for anybody to be curious or anxious on this account. Since Giribala was ten years old and Sashibhushan was a newly-fledged M.A., B.L. They were neighbours only.

Giribala's father Harakumar was at one time the sub-landlord of his village. Falling on evil days, he had sold everything and accepted the post of manager of their absentee landlord. He had to superintend the same *pargana* in which he lived, so that he was not obliged to move from his home.

Sashibhushan had taken his M.A. degree and also passed his examination in law, but he did not take up any work for a living. He could not bring himself to mix with people or speak even a few words at a meeting. Because of his short sight he could not recognize his acquaintances, hence he had to resort to frowning, which people considered a sign of arrogance.

It is all very well to keep oneself to oneself in the sea of humanity of a city like Calcutta; but in a village such behaviour is looked upon as haughtiness. When after many unsuccessful efforts, Sashibhushan's father at length sent his good-for-nothing son to look after their small village estate, Sashibhushan had to put up with a lot of ill-treatment, harassment and ridicule from his village neighbours. There was another reason for this persecution; peace-loving Sashibhushan was unwilling to marry—hence the worried parents of marriageable girls looked upon this unwillingness of his as intolerable pride and could not find it in their hearts to forgive him.

The more Sashibhushan was persecuted the more he hid himself in his den. He used to sit on a plank bed in a corner room with some bound English volumes before him and read whichever one he liked. This was all the work he did, and how the property managed to exist, the property alone knew.

We have already seen that Giribala was the only human being with whom he had any contact.

Giribala's brothers used to go to school and on their return would ask their silly little sister some day what the shape of the earth was; another day they would want to know which was bigger, the sun or the earth. And when she made mistakes, they corrected her with infinite contempt. If in the absence of proof to the contrary, Giribala considered the belief that the sun was bigger than the earth to be groundless, and if she had the boldness to express her doubts, then her brothers would declare with redoubled scorn, "Indeed! it is written in our books, and you—".

When Giribala heard that this fact was recorded in printed books, she was completely silenced and did not think any other proof necessary.

But she felt a great desire to be able to read books like her brothers. Some days she would sit in her own room with an open book before her, and go on muttering to herself as if she were reading, and keep turning over the pages quickly one after another. The small black unknown letters seemed to be keeping guard at the lion's gate of some great hall of mystery in endless serried rows, with bayonets of vowels raised aloft on their shoulders, and gave no reply to the questions put by Giribala. The Book of Fables revealed not a single word of its tigers, foxes, horses and donkeys to the curiosity-tormented girl, and the Book of Tales with all its tales remained gazing dumbly as if under a vow of silence.

Giribala had suggested taking lessons from her brothers, but they had not paid the slightest heed to her request. Sashibhushan was her sole ally.

Like the Fables and The Book of Tales, Sashibhushan also at first seemed to Giribala to be full of inscrutable mystery. The young man used to sit alone in the small sitting-room with iron-grated windows by the roadside, on a plank bed surrounded by books. Standing outside and catching hold of the bars Giribala would fix a wondering gaze upon this strange figure with bent back, absorbed in reading; and comparing the number of books, would decide in her own mind that Sashibhushan was much more learned than her brothers. She could conceive of nothing more wonderful than this.

She had not the slightest doubt that Sashibhushan had read through all the world's greatest books, such as the Book of Fables, etc. Hence when Sashibhushan turned over the pages, she stood stock-still, unable to measure the depths of his learning.

At length this wonderstruck girl came to attract the attention even of the short-sighted Sashibhushan. One day he opened a glittering bound volume and said, "Giribala, come and look at the pictures." Giribala immediately ran away.

This is how their acquaintance started, and it would require some historical research to determine the exact date on which it ripened into intimacy and the girl, entering Sashibhushan's room from outside the grating, obtained a seat amongst the bound books on the plank bed.

Giribala began taking lessons from Sashibhushan. My readers will laugh when they hear that this teacher taught his little pupil not only her letters, spelling and grammar, but translated and read out many great poems to her and asked her opinion of them. God alone knows what the girl understood but that she liked it, there is no doubt. She drew many imaginary and wonderful pictures in her child-mind made up of a mixture of understanding and non-understanding, and she listened intently and silently with wide-open eyes, asked one or two altogether foolish questions now and then, and sometimes veered off suddenly to an irrelevant subject. Sashibhushan never objected to this, but derived a particular pleasure from hearing this tiny little critic praise and blame and comment on famous poems. Giribala was his only discerning friend in the whole neighbourhood.

When Sashibhushan first came to know her, Giri was eight years old; now she was ten. In these two years, she had learnt the English and Bengali alphabet, and finished reading three or four easy books. At the same time Sashi-bhushan also had not felt these two years of village life to be altogether lonely and uninteresting.

3

But Sashibhushan had not been able to get on well with Giribala's father Harakumar. Harakumar used to come and ask this M.A., B.L. to advise him about his lawsuits. The said M.A., B.L., however, did not show much interest, nor did he hesitate to confess his ignorance of law to the Manager Babu, who considered this to be pure evasion. In this way two years passed.

At about this time, it had become imperative to punish a recalcitrant tenant. The Manager Babu earnestly entreated Sashibhushan to advise him with regard to his intention of prosecuting the said tenant in different districts on different charges and claims. But far from advising him, Sashibhushan said certain things to him quietly yet firmly, which did not strike him as being at all pleasant.

On the other hand Harakumar was unable to win a single case against this tenant, so he became firmly convinced that Sashibhushan had been helping the unfortunate man and vowed that the village should be rid of such a person without delay.

Sashibhushan found that cows kept straying into his fields, his pulse-stores were catching fire, his boundaries were being disputed, his tenants were making difficulties about paying their rents and not only that, were trying to bring false cases against him. There were even rumours that he would get a beating if he went out in the evenings, and his house would be set on fire some night.

At last the harmless peace-loving Sashibhushan prepared to leave the village and escape to Calcutta.

Whilst he was making his preparations, the Joint Magistrate Sahib's tents were pitched in the village, which thereupon became astir with constables, *khansamas*, dogs, horses, syces and sweepers. Batches of small boys began to wander about the outskirts of the Sahib's camp with fearful curiosity, like packs of jackals on a tiger's trail.

The Manager Babu proceeded to supply fowls, eggs, *ghee* and milk to the Sahib under the heading of hospita-lity, according to custom. He freely and unquestioningly supplied a much larger quantity of food than was actually required by the Joint Sahib; but when the Sahib's sweeper came one morning and demanded four seers of *ghee* at once for the Sahib's dog, then, as ill-luck would have it, Harakumar felt this was the limit and explained to the sweeper that though the Sahib's dog could doubtlessly digest much more *ghee* than a country dog without fear of consequences, still such a large quantity of fat was not good for its health; and he refused to supply the *ghee*.

The sweeper went and told the Sahib that he had gone to enquire from the Manager Babu where dog's meat could be had, but because he belonged to the sweeper caste the Manager had driven him away with contempt before everybody, and had not even hesitated to show disrespect to the Sahib.

As a rule Sahibs are easily offended by the Brahmin's pride of caste, moreover, they had dared to insult his sweeper; so that he found it impossible to control his temper, and immediately ordered his *chaprassi* to send for the Manager Babu.

The trembling Manager came and stood before the Sahib's tent, inwardly muttering the name of the goddess Durga. Coming out of the tent with loud creaking of boots, the Sahib shouted at the Manager in Bengali with a foreign accent: "Why have you driven away my sweeper?"

The flurried Harakumar hastened to assure the Sahib with folded hands that he could never dare to be so insolent as to drive away the Sahib's sweeper, but since the latter had asked for four seers of *ghee* at once for the dog, he (the Manager) had at first entered a mild protest in the interests of the said quadruped, and then sent out messengers to various places for procuring the *ghee*.

The Sahib enquired who had been sent out and where.

Harakumar promptly mentioned some names haphazard as they occurred to him.

The Sahib despatched messengers at once to enquire whether the aforesaid persons had been sent to the aforesaid villages to procure *ghee* and meanwhile kept the Manager Babu waiting in his tent.

The messengers came back in the afternoon and informed the Sahib that nobody had been sent anywhere for the *ghee*. This left no doubt in his mind that everything the Manager had said was false and his sweeper had spoken the truth. Whereupon, roaring with rage, the Joint Sahib called the sweeper and said, "Catch hold of this swine by the ear and race him round the tent", which command the sweeper executed in front of the crowd of spectators, without waste of time.

The report of this event spread like wild fire through the village and Harakumar came home and lay down like one half dead, without touching a morsel of food.

The Manager had made many enemies in connection with his *zemindari* work. They were overjoyed at the news, but when the departing Sashibhushan heard it, his blood boiled within him, and he could not sleep the whole night.

Next morning he went to Harakumar's house; the latter caught hold of his hand and began to weep bitterly. Sashibhushan said, "A case for libel must be brought against the Sahib, and I will fight it as your counsel."

At first Harakumar was frightened to hear that a suit must be filed against the Magistrate Sahib himself, but Sashibhushan strongly insisted upon it.

Harakumar asked for time to think it over. But when he found that the rumour had spread throughout the village and his enemies were openly expressing their jubilation, he hesitated no longer, and appealed to Sashibhushan, saying "My boy, I hear you are preparing to go to Calcutta for no ostensible reason—but you can't possibly do so. It is such a tower of strength for us to have a person like you in the village! Anyhow you must deliver me from this terrible indignity."

4

That Sashibhushan who had hitherto always tried to lead a guarded and secluded life screened from the public eye, it was that same Sashibhushan who now presented himself in court. On hearing his case, the Magistrate took him into his private chamber, and treated him with the utmost courtesy, saying "Sashi Babu, wouldn't it be better to compromise this case privately?"

Keeping his short-sighted frowning gaze fixed very steadily upon the cover of a law-book lying on the table

Sashi Babu replied, "I cannot advise my client to do so. How can he make a compromise privately when he has been insulted publicly?"

After exchanging a few words, the Sahib realized that this myopic and laconic young man was not to be easily moved and said, "All right Babu, let's see how it turns out in the end."

Saying which, the Magistrate adjourned the case and went on tour to the moffussil.

On the other hand, the Joint Sahib wrote as follows to the Zemindar: "Your Manager has insulted my servants and shown disrespect to me. I trust you will take necessary action."

The Zemindar was thoroughly upset and sent for Harakumar at once. The Manager recounted the whole affair in detail, from beginning to end. The Zemindar got extremely annoyed and said, "When the Sahib's sweeper asked for four seers of *ghee,* why didn't you give it to him at once without any question? Would it have cost you your father's money?"

Harakumar couldn't deny that his paternal property would not have suffered any loss thereby. Admitting he was to blame, he said, "It was my bad luck that made me act so foolishly."

"Then again, who told you to prosecute the Sahib", asked the Zemindar.

"O Incarnation of Righteousness", replied Harakumar, "I had no wish to prosecute: it was that young fellow Sashi of our village, who never gets a single brief—who got me into this mess by insisting upon it, almost without my permission."

Whereupon the Zemindar became highly incensed with Sashibhushan. He gathered that the aforesaid youth was a worthless new pleader, who was trying to attract the public eye by creating a sensation. He ordered the Manager to withdraw the case, and appease the pair of magistrates, elder and younger, immediately.

The Manager presented himself at the Joint Magistrate's quarters with a peace-offering of fruits and sweets calculated to cool the atmosphere. He informed the Sahib that it was altogether foreign to his nature to bring a case against him; it was only that green young duffer of a pleader known as Sashibhushan of their village who had the impudence to act thus, practically without his knowledge. The Sahib was exceedingly annoyed with Sashibhushan and extremely pleased with the Manager, whom he was *dukkhit* to have given *dandobidhan* in a fit of temper. The Sahib had recently won a prize in a Bengali examination, hence he was given to speaking in high-flown bookish language with all and sundry.

The Manager averred that parents sometimes punished their children in anger, at others drew them into their affectionate embrace, so that there was no occasion for either the parents or the children to feel sorry.

Whereupon, after distributing adequate largesse to all the Joint Sahib's servants, Harakumar went to the moffussil to see the Magistrate Sahib. After hearing all about Sashibhushan's arrogant behaviour from him, the Magistrate remarked, "It struck me also as very strange that the Manager Babu whom I had always thought to be such a nice person, instead of informing me first and arranging for private compromise, should rush to bring a suit. The whole thing seemed so preposterous! Now I understand everything."

Finally he asked the Manager whether Sashibhushan had joined the Congress. Without turning a hair the latter calmly replied, "Yes".

The Sahib's normal ruling-race complex led him to perceive clearly that this was all the Congress' doing. The myrmidons of the Congress were secretly going about everywhere seeking for opportunities to engineer trouble and write articles in the *Amrit Bazar* picking a quarrel with the Government. The Sahib inwardly cursed the Government of India's weakness in not giving more summary powers to the Magistrates to crush these puny thorns underfoot forthwith. But the name of Sashibhushan the Congressman remained in the Magistrate's memory.

5

When the big things of life raise their powerful heads, the small things also are not deterred from spreading their hungry little network of roots and putting forward their claim in the affairs of the world.

When Sashibhushan was particularly busy with the Magistrate's annoying case, when he was collecting notes on law from various volumes, sharpening in his mind the points he would make in his speech, cross-examining imaginary witnesses, and trembling and perspiring every now and again at the mental picture of the crowded court-room and the future sequence of cantos in his war-epic—then his little pupil used to come regularly to his door, shabby reader and ink-stained exercise-book in hand, sometimes with flowers and fruit, sometimes with pickles, coconut-sweets and spiced home-made catechu with the fragrance of the *ketaki* from her mother's store-room.

The first few days she noticed that Sashibhushan was absent-mindedly turning over the pages of a huge forbidding-looking volume without pictures, but it did not seem as if he was reading it very attentively either. Sashibhushan used to try and explain to Giribala some portion at least of the books he read on other occasions—were there then not even a few words in that heavy black-bound volume which he could read out to her? And in any case, was that book so very important and Giribala so very insignificant?

At first, in order to attract her preceptor's attention Giribala began to spell and read her lessons out aloud in a sing-song tone, swaying the upper half of her body including her plait, violently to and fro. But she found this plan did not work very well. She became intensely annoyed in her own mind with that heavy black book, which she began to look upon as an ugly, hard, cruel human being. Every unintelligible page of that book took on the form of a wicked man's face and silently expressed its utter contempt of Giribala, because she was a little girl. If some thief could have stolen that book, she would have rewarded him with all the spiced catechu in her mother's store-room. The gods did not listen to all the unreasonable and impossible prayers she mentally said to them for the destruction of that book, nor do I think it necessary for my readers to hear them either.

Then the dejected girl gave up going to her tutor's home, lesson-book in hand, for a day or two. On coming to the path in front of Sashibhushan's room to see the result of these two days of separation, and glancing inside, she found that Sashibhushan, putting aside the black book, was standing alone and addressing the iron bars in some foreign language with gesticulations.

Probably he was experimenting on those irons how to melt the heart of the judge.

Sashibhushan the bookworm, ignorant of the ways of the world, thought it not altogether impossible even in these mercenary days to perform the wonderful feats of orators like Demosthenes, Cicero, Burke, Sheridan, etc., who by the piercing arrows of their winged words had torn injustice to shreds, cowed down the tyrant, and humbled pride to the dust in the olden days. Standing in the small dilapidated house of Tilkuchi village, Sashibhushan was practising how to put to shame the arrogant English race flushed with the wine of victory, and make them repent for their misdeeds before the whole world. Whether the gods in heaven laughed to hear him or whether their divine eyes moistened with tears, nobody knows.

So he failed to notice Giribala. On that day the girl had no plums in her *sāri*-end. Having been caught once in the act of throwing plum-stones, she had become very sensitive with regard to that fruit, so much so that if Sashibhushan innocently asked some day— "Giri, are there no plums for me today?" she took it to be a veiled taunt and prepared to run away with the reproving exclamation "*jah!*" on her lips.

In the absence of plum-stones, she had to take recourse to a trick today. Suddenly looking at a distant point, she cried, "Swarna, dear, don't go, I shall be coming in a minute."

My masculine readers may think that these words were addressed to some distant companion, but my feminine readers will easily surmise that there was nobody in the distance and that the object aimed at was close at hand. But alas! the shot missed the blind man. Not that Sashibhushan had not heard, but he failed to perceive the purport of the call. He thought that the girl was really anxious to go and play and he had not the energy that day to draw her away from play to study, because he also was trying to aim his sharp arrows at somebody's heart. Just as the trifling aim of the girl's small hand missed the mark, so did the high aim of his practised hand, as my readers already know.

Plum-stones have this advantage that they can be thrown several times and if four miss the mark, then the fifth has a chance of hitting it. But however imaginary a person Swarna may be, she cannot be kept standing for long after one has told her "I am coming." If one treats her so, then people may naturally begin to entertain doubts as to her existence. So when this means failed, Giribala had to go without further delay. Still one did not notice in her steps that celerity which a sincere desire to join a distant companion would have warranted. It was as if she were trying to feel with her back whether anyone was following her or not; when she knew for certain that nobody was coming, then with a last feeble fraction of hope she looked round once, and not seeing anyone tore to pieces both that tiny hope and her loose-leaved lesson-book and scattered them on the road. If she could have found some possible means of returning the little knowledge that Sashibhushan had imparted to her, then probably she would have thrown it all down with a bang at Sashibhushan's door like the unwanted plum-stones, and come away. The girl vowed that before she met Sashibhushan next, she would forget all her lessons and not be able to answer any question he put to her—not one, not one, not even a single one! And then! Then Sashibhushan would be served right.

Giribala's eyes filled with tears. She derived some small comfort in her aching heart from thinking how deeply repentant Sashibhushan would feel if she forgot all her lessons, and a spring of pity welled up in her imagination for that future wretched Giribala, who would forget everything she had learnt, simply for Sashibhushan's fault.

Clouds gathered in the sky, as they do every day in the rainy season. Giribala stood behind a roadside tree sobbing for wounded pride. Such idle tears are shed every day by many a girl; it was nothing worthy of note.

6

My readers are aware of the reasons why Sashibhushan's researches into the law and his essays in oratory proved fruitless. The case against the Magistrate was suddenly withdrawn. Harakumar was appointed an Honorary Magistrate on the District bench and he used to go often to the district town in a soiled *chapkan* and greasy turban, to pay his respects to the Sahibs.

At long last Giribala's curses on that fat black book began to bear fruit—and it lay neglected, forgotten and exiled in a dark corner, collecting dust. But where was Giribala the girl who would have taken delight in this neglect?

The day when Sashibhushan closed his law-book and sat alone, he suddenly realized that Giribala had not come. Then he began to recollect the daily history of those few days, little by little. He remembered how one bright morning Giribala had brought a heap of *bakul* flowers wet with the new rains, tied in a corner of her *sāri*. When he did not raise his eyes from his book even on seeing her, her ardour became suddenly damped. Taking a needle-and-thread stuck in her *sāri*-end, she began to weave a garland of *bakul* flowers one by one, with bent head. She wove it very slowly, and it took a long time to finish; the day began to wear on, it was time for Giribala to go home, and yet Sashibhushan had not finished reading. Giribala left the garland on the plank bed, and sorrowfully went away. He remembered how her wounded feelings gradually gained in depth every day; how the time came when she gave up entering his room, and would appear now and again on the footpath in front and go away; and how at last the girl had even given up coming to the path—that too was now some days ago. Giribala's fit of pique never used to last so long. Sashibhushan sighed and remained sitting with his back against the wall like one bewildered and with nothing to do. In the absence of his little pupil, his books became distasteful to him.

He kept pulling one or two books towards him, then pushing them away again after reading two or three pages. If he began to write, his expectant eyes would throw an eager glance every now and again towards the lane and the house opposite, and his writing would be interrupted.

Sashibhushan was afraid Giribala had fallen ill. On making discreet enquiries, however, he learnt that his fears were groundless. Giribala did not go out of the house nowadays. A bridegroom had been settled for her.

On the morning following the day on which Giribala had strewn the muddy village lane with the torn leaves of her lesson-book, she was leaving the house early with quick steps, bearing various presents tied in her little *sari*-corner. Having passed a sleepless night owing to the intense heat, Harakumar was sitting outside with bared body, pulling at his *hookah,* since early morning. "Where are you going?" he asked Giri. "To Sashidada's house", she replied. "You needn't go to Sashibhushan's house", scolded Harakumar, "go back home." Saying which he spoke long and sternly to her anent the shameless behaviour of a grown-up girl about to enter her father-in-law's house. Since that day she had been forbidden to leave the house. This time she found no opportunity of humbling her pride and making it up with Sashibhushan. Mango-preserves, spiced catechu and pickled limes were relegated to their proper place on the store-room shelf. It went on raining, the *bakul* flowers went on falling, the guava-trees became laden with ripe fruit, and the ground beneath the plum trees became littered every day with succulent black plums dropped from the branches by pecking birds. Alas! even the loose-leaved lesson-book was no longer there.

7

On the day when the *sanai* was playing in the village for Giribala's wedding, the uninvited Sashibhushan was going to Calcutta by boat.

Since the withdrawal of the lawsuit the very sight of Sashibhushan had become a curse to Harakumar, for he was certain in his own mind that Sashibhushan looked down upon him with contempt. He began to discover a thousand imaginary proofs of this in Sashibhushan's looks and behaviour. All the other village-folk were gradually forgetting the history of his past indignity, only Sashibhushan was keeping alive its memory, he thought; hence he could not bear him. Whenever he met him, he used to feel a kind of shrinking shame, accompanied by a strong resentment. He vowed to himself that he would drive Sashibhushan out of the village.

It was not a very difficult task to constrain a person like Sashibhushan to leave the village. So the Manager Babu's desire was soon fulfilled. One morning Sashibhushan got into a boat with a load of books and a few tin boxes. The one happy tie that had bound him to the village, even that was being snapped today with great *éclat*. He had not fully realized before how firmly that delicate bond had entwined itself around his heart. Today when the boat set off, when the tops of the village trees and the sound of the wedding-music became gradually more and more indistinct, then suddenly a mist of tears spread over his heart and choked his voice, a rush of blood caused the veins in his forehead to throb with pain, and the whole panorama of the world seemed exceedingly hazy as if composed of shadowy illusion.

A strong wind was blowing from the opposite direction; hence the boat advanced slowly, though the current was favourable. At this juncture something happened on the river, which hindered Sashibhushan's journey.

A new steamer line had recently been opened from the station landing-place to the district town. Their steamer came noisily puffing along against the current, with its propellers working like wings and setting up waves on either side. The young Manager Sahib of the new line and a few passengers were on board, among whom were some inhabitants of Sashibhushan's village.

A money-lender's country-boat was trying to race the steamer from a little way off; at times it seemed about to catch up with her, and again kept falling behind. The boatman's spirit of rivalry was awakened. He put out a second sail on top of the first one, and even a third small sail atop of that. The tall mast bent low before the blast, and the parted waves danced madly with a loud splashing noise, on either side of the boat. The boat plunged forward like a horse with its reins snapped. At a certain point the path of the steamer took a slight bend, and here the boat outstripped it by taking a shorter cut. The Manager Sahib was leaning over the railing, eagerly watching this race. When the boat was flying along at top speed and had outstripped the steamer by about a yard, just then the Sahib raised his revolver and fired a shot at the swollen sail. In a moment the sail burst, the boat sank, and the steamer was hidden from sight round the bend.

Why the Manager acted thus, it is difficult to say. We Bengalis cannot always understand the workings of the Sahib's mind. Perhaps he felt the rivalry of an Indian sail to be intolerable; perhaps there is a fierce pleasure in putting a bullet through something broad and swollen in the twinkling of an eye; perhaps there is a certain ferocious and fiendish humour in putting the proud boat *hors de combat* in a second by making a few holes in its cloth. What the reason was I do not know exactly. But this I know for certain that the Englishman believed he would not be liable to be punished for this little joke, and he had an idea that the people whose boat was lost and who were in danger of losing their lives also could not be counted as human beings.

When the Sahib fired and the boat sank, Sashibhushan's boat had approached the place of occurrence. Sashibhushan was an eye-witness of the last scene. He hastened to the spot with his boat and rescued the boatmen. Only the man who was grinding spices for cooking in the kitchen could not be traced. The rain-swollen river flowed on swiftly.

The hot blood boiled in Sashibhushan's veins. The law was very dilatory—like a huge complex iron machine; it accepted proofs after weighing them, and apportioned punishment calmly—it did not possess the warmth of the human heart. But to separate food from hunger, desire from enjoyment, and anger from punishment appeared to Sashibhushan to be equally unnatural. There are many crimes which as soon as witnessed demand an immediate retribution from the witness' own hand, otherwise the god in him seems to sear the witness from within. At such a moment one feels inwardly ashamed to find comfort in the idea of the law. But the machine-made law and the machine-made steamer took the Manager further away from Sashibhushan. Whether the world was benefited in other ways, I cannot say, but this much is certain that Sashibhushan's Indian spleen was saved at this juncture.

Sashibhushan returned to the village with the boatmen who had survived. The boat had been laden with jute, which he appointed men to salvage, and tried to persuade the boatman to bring a police-case against the Manager.

But the boatman was unwilling to do so. He said the boat was sunk for good, but he was not prepared to sink with it. First of all, he would have to grease the palms, of the police; then he would have to give up all work and food and rest and wander about the law-courts; then God alone knows what trouble was in store for him and what the result would be if he prosecuted the Sahib. At last when he heard that Sashibhushan was himself a pleader, that he himself would pay all the costs of the suit and that there was every chance of his getting damages, he agreed. But the people of Sashibhushan's village who were present on board the steamer flatly refused to bear witness. "We didn't see anything, sir", they said to Sashibhushan, "we were at the back of the steamer, it was impossible to hear a gunshot for the throbbing of the machine and the lapping of the water."

Inwardly cursing his countrymen, Sashibhushan continued to conduct the case before the Magistrate.

No witnesses were required. The Manager admitted he had fired a shot. He said it was aimed at a flock of cranes flying in the sky. The steamer was then going at full speed and had just turned round the bend. So he could not possibly know whether a crow died or a crane died or the boat sank. Earth and sky contained so many things to aim at that no man in his senses would knowingly waste a pice-worth of shot on a dirty rag.

Acquitted on all charges, the Manager Sahib, puffing at a cigar, went to play whist at his club. The dead body of the man who was grinding spices in the boat was washed up on land nine miles farther off, and Sashibhushan returned to his village with frustration raging in his breast.

The day he returned, they were taking Giribala to her husband's home in a decorated boat. Though nobody had asked him, yet Sashibhushan came slowly to the riverside. The landing-place was crowded, so instead of going there he stood a little way off. When the boat left the landing-steps and passed in front of him, he caught a fleeting glimpse of the new bride, sitting with her *sari* drawn down over her bowed head. Giribala had long been hoping to see Sashibhushan somehow or other before leaving the village, but today she did not even know that her preceptor was standing there not very far away. She did not even raise her head once to look; only the tears coursed down both her cheeks in silent weeping.

The boat gradually receded and passed out of sight. The morning light glittered on the river; from the branch of a mango-tree nearby, a *papia* burst into rapturous song every now and then, seeking in vain to unburden the passion of its heart; the ferry-boat, laden with passengers, kept plying from one side of the river to the other; the women coming to the landing-steps to draw water, began discussing Giri's departure for her father-in-law's house in a loud babel of voices; and Sashibhushan, taking off his glasses and wiping his eyes, turned back and entered the small iron-grated room by the roadside. Suddenly it seemed as if he heard Giribala's voice calling "Sashidada!"

—Where, oh where?

Nowhere! Not in the room, not in the lane, not in the village—but in the midst of his own heart.

8

Sashibhushan again packed up his things and started for Calcutta. He had nothing to do in Calcutta, there was no particular object in going there; so instead of going by rail, he decided to travel all the way by boat.

At the height of the rainy season, a network of big and small zig-zag waterways had spread over the whole of Bengal. The veins and arteries of this green land seemed to be overflowing with sap on all sides into trees and plants, bushes and grass, corn and jute and sugarcane, in a mad exuberance of riotous youth.

Sashibhushan's boat proceeded to thread its way through all these narrow serpentine alleys of water, which had by then become level with the bank. The white-tufted grass and reeds and in some places the cornfields were under water. The bamboo-groves and mango-groves and fencing of the village had reached the very edge of the river, as if the daughters of the gods had filled with water to the brink the circular grooves around the tree-roots.

When he set out the woods were bright and smiling and glistening after their bath; but it soon clouded over and began to rain; whichever way one turned, it looked dismal and dingy. Just as during a flood, the cattle huddle together in their dirty, slushy, narrow byre and get drenched in the incessant showers of July, standing patiently with pathetic eyes; so was the harassed countryside of Bengal, dumb and sorrowful, being soaked continuously in its dense swamped and slippery jungles. The peasants were going about with their palm-leaf umbrellas; the women were going from one hut to another in the course of their daily household duties, getting drenched and shrinking from the cold wet wind and treading the slippery landing-stairs very cautiously to draw water from the river in their wet clothes. The men were sitting in their verandahs smoking, or if absolutely necessary, going out with *chaddar* wound round the waist, umbrellas over their heads and shoes in their hands. It is not one of our ancient and sacred customs to provide our long-suffering womenfolk with umbrellas in this sunburnt and rain-swept land of Bengal.

When the rain showed no signs of stopping, Sashi-bhushan began to get tired of the closed boat, and again decided to travel by rail. Arriving at a wide confluence of the river, he moored the boat and began to prepare for his midday meal.

It is the lame man's foot that falls into the ditch, as the saying goes. It is not the fault of the ditch alone, but the lame man's foot also has a special bent for falling into the ditch. On that day Sashibhushan furnished a good proof of this.

The fishermen had fixed bamboo-poles on either side of the confluence of two rivers and spread a huge net over them, keeping only room on one side for boats to pass. They had been doing this since a long time, and also paying rent for it. As ill luck would have it, this year the august District Superintendent of Police had suddenly deigned to come this way. Seeing his boat draw near, the fishermen warned his boatman beforehand in a loud voice and pointed out the passage at the side. But the Sahib's boatman was not in the habit of showing deference to any man-made barrier by taking a roundabout route, so he steered the boat clean through the net. The net stooped and made way for the boat, but its rudder became enmeshed and it took some time and trouble to disentangle it.

The Police Sahib got extremely red and angry, and had the boat moored. The four fishermen, seeing his threatening attitude, promptly decamped. The Sahib ordered his oarsmen to cut up the net, and the huge net, made at a cost of seven or eight hundred rupees, was cut to pieces.

After venting his wrath on the net, the Sahib finally sent for the fishermen. Unable to find the four runaway men, the constable caught hold of whichever four fishermen came to hand. They pleaded their innocence with folded hands supplicatingly. As the Police Bahadur was giving orders to his men to take the prisoners along with them, the bespectacled Sashibhushan with an unbuttoned shirt hastily thrown over his shoulders and his slippers pattering on the ground came in breathless haste to the police boat. In a quivering voice he said, "Sir, you have no right to cut up the net of these fishermen, and to harass these four men."

As soon as the Burra Sahib of the Police uttered a particularly offensive invective in Hindi, Sashibhushan sprang into the boat from the slightly raised river-bank, and throwing himself at once upon the Sahib, began to pummel him right and left like a child, like a madman.

After that he did not know what happened. When he awoke in the police-station, we are constrained to say that the treatment he received was conducive neither to his sense of dignity nor to his physical comfort.

9

Sashibhushan's father, with the assistance of pleaders and barristers, first got his son released on bail. Then preparations were set afoot for conducting the case.

The fishermen whose net had been destroyed belonged to the same holding and were under the same zemindar as Sashibhushan. When in difficulty, they used to come to him sometimes for legal advice. The men who had been seized and brought to the boat by the Sahib were also not unknown to him.

Sashibhushan sent for them in order to cite them as witnesses, but they were frightened out of their wits. If those who had to pass their daily lives with wife and children were to quarrel with the police, then where would their troubles end? How many lives were there in one man's body? The loss they had suffered was over and done with, now why this further trouble of a subpoena for bearing witness! "Sir, you have landed us in a great mess!" they all declared.

After much persuasion, they agreed to tell the truth.

In the meantime, when Harakumar took the opportunity of sitting on the bench to go and *salaam* the Sahibs, the Police Sahib said with a smile, "Manager Babu, I hear your tenants are ready to bear false witness against the police."

"Indeed! is such a thing possible?" said the startled manager, "that the sons of swine should have it in their bones to dare to do a thing like that!"

Readers of newspapers know that Sashibhushan's case had no legs to stand on.

One by one the fishermen came and deposed that the Sahib had not cut up their net, but had sent for them to the boat and taken down their names and addresses.

Not only that, but three or four of his village acquaintances stated that they were present at the place and time of occurrence, as members of a wedding-party, and had seen with their own eyes how Sashibhushan without any provocation had come forward and harassed the police constables.

Sashibhushan admitted that on being abused he had jumped into the boat and struck the Sahib; but the real reason for that was the destruction of the net and the ill-treatment of the fishermen.

Under the circumstances, that Sashibhushan should be punished could not be called unjust. But the sentence was somewhat severe. There were three or four charges—assault, trespass, interfering with police officers on duty, etc.—all of which were fully proved against him.

Leaving his beloved books in that small room, Sashibhushan went to jail for five years. When his father wanted to appeal, Sashibhushan repeatedly forbade him to do so. "Jail is welcome", he said, "iron bonds don't lie, but the freedom we have outside deceives us and gets us into trouble. And if you talk of good company, then the liars and cowards in jail are comparatively fewer, because there is less room—outside their number is much larger."

10

Soon after Sashibhushan went to jail, his father died. He had hardly any relatives to speak of. A brother of his had been holding a post in the Central Provinces since a long time, and could not make it convenient to come home very often; he had built a house for himself and settled there with his family. Whatever property he had in his village home was mostly appropriated by the manager Harakumar on various pretexts.

Fate so willed it that Sashibhushan had to undergo much more suffering in jail than usually fell to the lot of prisoners. Still the five long years passed.

Again one rainy day Sashibhushan came and stood outside the prison-walls with ruined health and vacant mind. He had gained his freedom, and that was all he had: he had no one and nothing to call his own. With no home, no relatives and no friends, he felt that the vast world was too big and loose for his solitary self.

While he was deliberating where to begin to pick up the broken threads of his life, a big carriage and pair came and stood in front of him. A servant alighted and asked him, "Is your name Sashibhushan Babu?" "Yes", he replied.

The man immediately held open the carriage-door and waited for Sashibhushan to get in. "Where am I to go?" he asked in surprise.

"My master has sent for you", replied the servant.

As the curious looks of the passers-by were getting intolerable, Sashibhushan jumped into the carriage without more ado. Surely there must be some mistake, he thought to himself. But he had to go somewhere in any case, and a mistake might just as well serve as the prelude to a new life.

On that day also sunshine and clouds were chasing each other all over the sky; and the rainwashed dark green corn-fields skirting the road were chequered with the lively play of sun and shadow. There was a huge chariot lying near the market-place, and from a grocer's shop nearby some Vaishnava mendicants were singing to the accompaniment of string instruments, drums and cymbals:

> *Come back, come back! O lord of my heart,*
> *Beloved, come back to this hungry,*
> *parched and fevered breast.*

As the carriage advanced, the lines of the song could be heard growing fainter and still more faint in the distance:

> *O cruel one, come back! O soft and loving come!*
> *Come back, O thou of the tender hue of the rain*
> *cloud!*

The words of the song became gradually blurred and indistinct and could no longer be followed. But its rhythm had set up a turmoil in Sashibhushan's breast; he began humming to himself and adding line after line to the song, and seemed unable to stop:

O my joy, forever and forever my grief,

come back!

O treasure churned from all my grief and joy,

come to my heart.

O ever-desired, and ever-cherished one,

O thou fleeting, O thou everlasting,

come to my arms.

Come to my bosom, to my eyes, in my sleep,

in my dreams, in the clothes and jewels I wear,

to my whole world.

Come in the laughter of my lips, in the

tears of my eyes,

My caresses, my wiles, my wounded pride,

In every remembrance and in forgetfulness.

In my faith and my work, my love's

ardour and shyness,

In my life and my death, O come!

Sashibhushan's singing came to an end when the carriage entered a walled garden and stopped in front of a two-storeyed house.

Without asking any questions he followed the servant's directions and entered the house.

The room in which he came and sat was lined on all sides with big glass book cases filled with rows upon rows of books of various colours and various bindings.

At this sight his former life was set free from prison at once for the second time. These gilted and multi-coloured books seemed to him like familiar jewelled lion-gates at the entrance of the kingdom of joy.

There were some things lying on the table also. The short-sighted Sashibhushan bent forward and saw a cracked slate upon which were some old exercise books, a much torn arithmetic book, the Book of Fables and a Kashiram Das Mahabharata.

Upon the wooden frame of the slate was written in bold characters in Sashibhushan's hand—Giribala Devi. Upon the books and exercise books the same name was written in the same hand.

Now Sashibhushan knew where he had come. The blood coursed wildly in his veins. He looked out of the open window, and what did he see there? The small iron-barred room, the uneven village lane, the little girl in a striped *sāri*,—and his own carefree, quiet and peaceful daily life.

The happy life of those days was nothing wonderful nor extraordinary; day after day used to pass by unconsciously in trivial tasks and trivial joys, and the teaching of a little girl pupil was only one amongst those trifling things but that secluded life in a village corner, that circumscribed peace, those small joys, the face of that little girl—everything seemed to exist in a land of desire and shadowy imagination—in a heaven outside time and space and beyond his grasp.

All the scenes and memories of those bygone days, mingled with the soft light of this rainy morning and the *kirtan* song softly ringing in his ears, seemed to take on a new beauty of melodious sound and radiant light. The memory of the sad and hurt look on the face of the little neglected girl as he had last seen her in the jungle-girt muddy village lane was transformed on the canvas of his mind into a unique and wonderful picture full of deep pathos and a divine beauty. The sad tune of the *kirtan* blended with that picture, and it seemed to him that the ineffable sorrow at the heart of the universe had cast its shadow upon the face of that village maiden. Placing both arms on the slate and books upon the table, and hiding his face in them, Sashibhushan began after many years to dream dreams of long ago.

After a long time, hearing a slight noise Sashibhushan started and raised his head. He saw before him fruits and sweets on a silver salver, and at a little distance, Giribala standing and silently waiting. As soon as he looked up, Giribala, clad all in white in widow's garb, without a single ornament on her person, came and knelt before him, and took the dust of his feet.

She rose and looked at him—so emaciated and pale and broken in health—with her eyes full of sweet sympathy; and tears coursed down her cheeks.

Sashibhushan made an effort to ask her how she was, but could not find words to do so; stifled tears choked his utterance. The *kirtan* singers came and stood in front of the house in the course of their begging round and began to sing over and over again—

Come back, Beloved, come back!

Mahamaya

They met together in a ruined temple on the river bank: Mahamaya and Rajib.

In silence she cast her naturally grave look at Rajib with a tinge of reproach. It meant to say: "How durst you call me here at this unusual hour today? You have ventured to do it only because I have so long obeyed you in all things!"

Rajib had a little awe of Mahamaya at all times, and now this look of hers thoroughly upset him: he at once gave up his fondly conceived plan of making a set speech to her. And yet he had to give quickly some reason for this interview. So, he hurriedly blurted out, "I say, let us run away from this place and marry." True,

Rajib thus delivered himself of what he had had in his mind; but the preface he had silently composed was lost. His speech sounded very dry and bald—even absurd. He himself felt confused after saying it, and had no power left in him to add some words to modify its effect. The fool! After calling Mahamaya to that ruined temple by the riverside at midday, he could only tell her, "Come, let us marry!"

Mahamaya was a *kulin's* daughter, twenty-four years old—in the full bloom of her youth and beauty, like an image of pure gold, of the hue of the early autumn sunlight; radiant and still as that sunshine, with a gaze free and fearless as daylight itself.

She was an orphan. Her elder brother, Bhavanicharan Chattopadhyay, looked after her. The two were of the same mould—taciturn, but possessing a force of character which burnt silently like the midday sun. People feared Bhavanicharan without knowing why.

Rajib had come there from afar with the Burra Sahib of the silk factory of the place. His father had served this Sahib, and when he died, the Sahib underook to bring up his orphan boy and took him with himself to this Bamanhati factory. In those early days such instances of sympathy were frequent among the Sahibs. The boy was accompanied by his loving aunt, and they lived in Bhavanicharan's neighbourhood. Mahamaya was Rajib's playmate in childhood, and was dearly loved by his aunt.

Rajib grew up to be sixteen, seventeen, eighteen, and even nineteen; and yet, in spite of his aunt's constant urging, he refused to marry. The Sahib was highly pleased to hear of this uncommon instance of good sense in a Bengali youth, and imagined that Rajib had taken him as his ideal in life. I may here add that the Sahib was a bachelor. The aunt died soon after.

For Mahamaya, too, no bridegroom of an equal grade of blue blood could be secured except for an impossible dowry. She steadily grew up in maidenhood.

The reader hardly needs to be told that though the god who ties the marriage knot had so long been ignoring this young couple, the god who forms the bond of love had not been idle all this time. While old *Prajāpati* was dozing, young *Kandarpa* was very much awake.

Kandarpa's influence shows itself differently in different persons. Under his inspiration Rajib constantly sought for a chance of whispering his heart's longings, but Mahamaya never gave him such an opportunity; her silent and grave look sent a chill of fear through the wild heart of Rajib.

Today he had, by a hundred solemn entreaties and conjurations, at last succeeded in bringing her to this ruined temple. He had planned that he would today freely tell her all that he had to say and thereafter there would be for him either lifelong happiness or death in life. Yet at this crisis of his fate Rajib could only say, "Come, let us go and marry", and then he stood confused and silent like a boy who had forgotten his lesson.

For a long while she did not reply, as if she had never expected such a proposal from Rajib.

The noontide has many undefined plaintive notes of its own; these began to make themselves heard in the midst of that stillness. The broken door of the temple, half detached from its hinge, began at times to open and to close in the wind with a low wailing creak. The pigeon, perched on the temple window, began its deep booming. The wood-pecker kept up its monotonous noise as it sat working on the *shimul* branch outside. The lizard darted through the heaps of dry leaves with a rustling sound. A sudden gust of warm wind blowing from the fields passed through the trees, making all their foliage whistle. Of a sudden the river waters woke into ripple and lapped on the broken steps of the *ghat*. Amidst these stray, languid sounds came the rustic notes of a cow-boy's flute from a far-off tree-shade. Rajib stood reclining against the ruinous plinth of the temple like a tired dreamer, gazing at the river; he had not the spirit to look Mahamaya in the face.

After a while he turned his head and again cast a supplicating glance at Mahamaya's face. She shook her head and replied, "No, it can't be."

At once the whole fabric of his hopes was dashed to the ground; for he knew that when Mahamaya shook her head it was through her own convictions, and nobody else in the world could bend her to his own will. The high pride of pedigree had run in the blood of Mahamaya's family for untold generations—could she ever consent to marry a Brahmin of low pedigree like Rajib? To love is one thing, and to marry quite another. She, however, now realized that her own thoughtless conduct in the past had encouraged Rajib to hope so audaciously; and at once she prepared to leave the temple.

Rajib understood her, and quickly broke in with "I am leaving these parts tomorrow."

At first she thought of appearing indifferent to the news; but she could not. Her feet did not move when she wanted to depart. Calmly she asked, "Why?" Rajib replied, "My Sahib has been transferred from here to the Sonapur factory, and he is taking me with him." Again she stood in long silence, musing thus: 'Our lives are moving in two contrary directions. I cannot hope to keep a man a prisoner of my eyes for ever.' So she opened her compressed lips a little and said, "Very well." It sounded rather like a deep sigh.

With this word only she was again about to leave, when Rajib started up with the whisper "your brother!"

She looked out and saw her brother coming towards the temple, and she knew that he had found out their assignation. Rajib, fearing to place Mahamaya in a false position, tried to escape by jumping out of the hole in the temple wall; but Mahamaya seized his arm and kept him back by main force. Bhavanicharan entered the temple, and only cast one silent and placid glance at the pair.

Mahamaya looked at Rajib and said with an unruffled voice, "Yes, I will go to your house, Rajib. Do you wait for me."

Silently Bhavanicharan left the temple, and Mahamaya followed him as silently. And Rajib? He stood in a maze as if he had been doomed to death.

2

That very night Bhavanicharan gave a crimson silk *sāri* to Mahamaya and told her to put it on at once. Then he said, "Follow me". Nobody had ever disobeyed

Bhavanicharan's bidding or even his hint; Mahamaya herself was no exception to it.

That night the two walked to the burning-place on the river-bank, not far from their home. There in the hut for sheltering dying men brought to the holy river's side, an old Brahmin was lying in expectation of death. The two went up to his bedside. A Brahmin priest was present in one corner of the room; Bhavanicharan beckoned to him. The priest quickly got his things ready for the happy ceremony. Mahamaya realized that she was to be married to this dying man, but she did not make the least objection. In the dim room, faintly lit up by the glare of two funeral pyres hard by, the muttered sacred texts mingled with the groans of the dying as Mahamaya's marriage was celebrated.

The day following her marriage she became a widow. But she did not feel excessively grieved at the bereavement. And Rajib, too, was not so crushed by the news of her widowhood as he had been by the unexpected tridings of her marriage. Nay, he felt rather cheered. But this feeling did not last long. A second terrible blow laid him utterly in the dust; he heard that there was a grand ceremony at the burning *ghāt* that day as Mahamaya was going to burn herself with her husband's corpse.

At first he thought of informing his Sahib and forcibly stopping the cruel sacrifice with his help. But then he recollected that the Sahib had made over charge and left for Sonapur that very day; he had wanted to take Rajib with him, but the youth had stayed behind on a month's leave.

Mahamaya had told him "Wait for me". This request he must by no means disregard. He had at first taken a month's leave, but if need were he would take two months', then three months' leave and finally throw up the Sahib's service and live by begging, yet he would wait for her to his life's close.

Just when Rajib was going to rush out madly and commit suicide or some other terrible deed, a deluge of rain came down with a desolating storm at sunset. The tempest threatened to tumble his house down on his head. He gained some composure when he found that the convulsion in outer nature was harmonizing with the storm within his soul. It seemed to him that all Nature had taken up his cause and was going to bring him some sort of remedy. The force he wished to apply in his own person but could not was now being applied by Nature herself over earth and sky.

At such a time some one pushed the door hard from outside. Rajib hastened to open it. A woman entered the room, clad in a wet garment, with a long veil covering her entire face. Rajib at once knew her for Mahamaya.

In a voice full of emotion he asked, "Mahamaya, have you come away from the funeral pyre?"

She replied, "Yes, I had promised you to come to your house. Here I am, to keep my word. But, Rajib, I am not exactly the same person; I am changed altogether. I am the Mahamaya of old in my mind only. Speak now, I can yet go back to the funeral pyre. But if you swear never to draw my veil aside, never to look on my face, then I shall live in your house."

It was enough to get her back from the hand of Death; all other considerations vanished before it. Rajib promptly replied, "Live here in any fashion you like; if you leave me I shall die."

Mahamaya said, "Then come away at once. Let us go where your Sahib has gone on transfer."

Abandoning all his property in that house, Rajib went forth into the midst of the storm with Mahamaya. The force of the wind made it hard for them to stand erect; the gravel driven by the wind pricked their limbs like buck shot. The two took to the open fields, lest the trees by the roadside should crash down on their heads. The violence of the wind struck them from behind, as if the tempest had torn the couple as under from human habitations and was blowing them away on to destruction.

3

The reader must not discredit my tale as false or supernatural. There are traditions of a few such occurrences having taken place in the days when the burning of widows was customary.

Mahamaya had been bound hand and foot and placed on the funeral pyre, to which fire was applied at the appointed time. The flames had shot up from the pile, when a violent storm and rainshower began. Those who had come to conduct the cremation quickly fled for refuge to the hut for dying men and shut the door. The rain put the funeral fire out in no time. Meantime the bands on Mahamaya's wrists had been burnt to ashes, setting her hands free. Without uttering a groan amidst the intolerable pain of burning, she sat up and untied her feet. Then wrapping round herself her partly burnt cloth, she rose half-naked from the pyre, and first came to her own house. There was no one there; all had gone to the burning *ghāt*. She lighted a lamp, put on a fresh cloth, and looked at her face in a glass.

Dashing the mirror down on the ground, she mused for a while. Then she drew a long veil over her face and went to Rajib's house which was hard by. The reader knows what happened next.

True, Mahamaya now lived in Rajib's house, but there was no joy in his life. It was not much, but only a simple veil that parted the one from the other. And yet that veil was eternal like death, but more agonizing than death itself; because despair in time deadens the pang of death's separation, while a living hope was being daily and hourly crushed by the separation which that veil caused.

For one thing there was a spirit of motionless silence in Mahamaya from of old; and now the hush from within the veil appeared doubly unbearable. She seemed to be living within a winding sheet of death. This silent death clasped the life of Rajib and daily seemed to shrivel it up. He lost the Mahamaya whom he had known of old, and at the same time this veiled figure ever sitting by his side silently prevented him from enshrining in his life the sweet memory of her as she was in her girlhood. He brooded: 'Nature has placed barrier enough between one human being and another. Mahamaya, in particular, has been born, like Karua of old, with a natural charm against all evil. There is an innate fence round her being. And now she seems to have been born a second time and come to me with a second line of fences round herself. Ever by my side, she yet has become so remote as to be no longer within my reach. I am sitting outside the inviolable circle of her magic and trying, with an unsatiated thirsty soul, to penetrate this thin but unfathomable mystery, as the stars wear out the hours night after night in the vain attempt to pierce the mystery of the 'dark night with their sleepless winkless downcast gaze.'

Long did these two companionless lonely creatures thus pass their days together.

One night, on the tenth day of the new moon, the clouds withdrew for the first time in that rainy season, and the moon showed herself. The motionless moonlit night seemed to be sitting in a vigil by the head of the sleeping world. That night Rajib too had quitted his bed and sat gazing out of his window. From the heat-oppressed woodland a peculiar scent and the lazy hum of the cricket were entering into his room. As he gazed, the sleeping tank by the dark rows of trees glimmered like a polished silver plate. It is hard to say whether man at such a time thinks any clearly defined thought. Only his heart rushes in a particular direction—it sends forth an effusion of odour like the woodland, it utters

a cricket hum like the night. What Rajib was thinking of I know not; but it seemed to him that that night all the old laws had been set aside; that day the rainy season's night had drawn aside her veil of clouds, and this night looked silent, beautiful and grave like the Mahamaya of those early days. All the currents of his being flowed impetuously together towards *that* Mahamaya.

Like one moving in a dream, Rajib entered Mahamaya's bedroom. She was asleep then.

He stood by her side and stooped down to gaze on her. The moonbeams had fallen on her face. But, Oh horror! where was that face known of old? The flame of the funeral pyre, with its ruthless greedy tongue, had utterly licked away a part of the beauty from the left cheek of Mahamaya and left there only the ravages of its hunger.

Did Rajib start? Did a muffled cry escape from his lips? Probably so. Mahamaya woke up with a start— and saw Rajib before her. At once she replaced her veil and stood erect, leaving her bed. Rajib knew that the thunderbolt was uplifted. He fell down before her— he clasped her feet, crying "forgive me!"

She answered not a word, she did not look back for a moment as she walked out of the room. She never

came back. No trace of her was found anywhere. The parting left all the remaining days of Rajib's life branded with a long scar.

The Conclusion

Apurba had got his B.A. degree and was coming back home to his village. The river, which flowed past it, was a small one. It became dried up during the hot weather, but now in the July monsoon the heavy rains had swollen its current and it was full to the brim.

The boat, which carried Apurba, reached the *ghāt* whence the roof of his home could be seen through the dense foliage of the trees. Nobody knew that he was coming and therefore there was no one to receive him at the landing. The boatman offered to carry his bag, but Apurba picked it up himself, and took a leap from the boat. The bank was slippery, and he fell flat upon the muddy stair, bag and all.

As he did so, peal after peal of very sweet laughter rose in the sky, and startled the birds in the neighbouring trees. Apurba got up and tried to regain his composure as best as he could. When he sought for the source of his discomfiture, he found, sitting upon a heap of bricks lately unloaded from some cargo boat, a girl shaking her sides with laughter. Apurba recognized her as Mrinmayi, the daughter of their neighbour. This family had built their former house some distance away, but the river shifted its course cutting away into the land; and they had been obliged to change their quarter and settle down in the village only about two years ago.

Mrinmayi was the talk of all the village. The men called her 'madcap', but the village matrons were in a state of perpetual anxiety becuase of her untractable wildness. All her games were with the boys of the place, and she had the utmost contempt for the girls of her own age. The favourite child of her father, she had got into these unmanageable ways. Her mother would often complain to her friends of her husband's spoiling the child. But, because she was well aware that the father would be cut to the quick if he saw his daughter in tears, the mother had not the heart to punish the girl herself.

Mrinmayi's face was more like that of a boy than a girl. Her short crop of curly hair reached down to her shoulders, and her big dark eyes showed no sign of fear or shyness. When the boat, carrying the absentee landlord of the village, was moored at the landing stage, she did not share the feeling of awe which possessed the neighbourhood, but shook her curly mane and took up a naked child in her arms and was the first to come and take her observation of the habits of this strange creature.

Apurba had come in touch with this girl on former occasions, and he had got into the habit of thinking about her from time to time during his leisure, and even while at work. Naturally, therefore, this laughter, with which she greeted his arrival, did not please him, in spite of its musical quality. He gave up his bag to the boatman and almost ran away towards his house. The whole setting of things was romantic—the river bank, the shade of the trees, the morning sunshine with birds' songs, and his youth of twenty years. The brick heaps hardly fitted in with the picture, but the girl who sat on the top of them made up for all deficiencies.

2

The widowed mother was beside herself with joy when her son returned unexpectedly. She at once sent her men to all parts of the village to search for milk and curds and fish. There was quite a stir among the neighbours. After the midday meal, the mother ventured to suggest to Apurba that he should turn his thoughts towards marriage. Apurba was prepared for this attack, as it had been tried before, and he had then put it off on the plea of examinations. But now that he had got his degree, he could have no such excuse to delay the inevitable. So he told his mother that if a suitable bride could be discovered he could then make up his mind.

The mother said that the discovery had been already made, and therefore there was no further excuse for deliberation. But Apurba was of opinion that deliberation was necessary, and insisted on seeing the girl before consenting to marry her. The mother agreed to this, though the request seemed superfluous.

The next day Apurba went out on his marriage expedition. The intended bride lived in a house which was not far from their own. Apurba took special care about his dress before starting. He put on his new silk suit and a fashionable turban much affected by the Calcutta people. He did not forget to display his patent leather shoes and silk umbrella. His reception was loudly cordial in the house of his would-be father-in-law. The little victim—the intended bride—was scrubbed and painted, beribboned and bejewelled, and brought before Apurba. She sat in a corner of the room, veiled up to her chin, with her head nearly touching her knees, and her middle-aged maidservant at her back to encourage her when in trouble. Her young brother sat near closely observing Apurba—his turban, his watch-chain, his newly budding moustache.

Apurba solemnly asked the girl: "What text-books are you reading in your school?"

No answer came from this bundle of bashfulness wrapped in coloured silk. After repeated questionings and secret pushings in the back by the maidservant, she rapidly gave the names of all her lesson-books in one breath.

Just at this moment the sound of scampering feet was heard outside and Mrinmayi burst into the room very much out of breath. She did not give the least heed to Apurba, but at once caught hold of the hand of Rakhal, the young brother, and tried to drag him outside. But Rakhal was intently engaged in cultivating his faculty of observation and refused to stir. The maidservant tried to scold Mrinmayi, keeping the pitch of her voice within the proper limits of decorum. Aparba retained his composure and sat still and sullen, fondling the watch-chain with his fingers.

When Mrinmayi failed in her attempt to make Rakhal move, she gave the boy a sounding smack on the shoulder, then she pulled up the veil from the face of the intended bride, and rushed out of the room like a miniature tornado. The maidservant growled and grumbled and Rakhal began to laugh immoderately at the sudden unveiling of his sister. He evidently did not take ill the blow he had received, because they had with each other a running account of such amenities. There was once a time when Mrinmayi had her hair long enough to reach her waist, and it was Rakhal who had ploughed his scissors through it one day till the girl in disgust had snatched them from the boy's hand and completed the destruction herself, leaving a mass of curls lying upon the dust like a bunch of black grapes.

After this cataclysm, the business of the examination came to a sudden stop. The girl-bride rose from her seat and changed from a circle of misery into a straight line, and then disappeared into the inner apartment. Apurba got up, still stroking his moustache, only to discover that his patent leather shoes had vanished. A great search was made for them, but they were nowhere to be found. There was nothing else to do but to borrow from the head of the house a pair of old slippers, which were sadly out of keeping with the rest of his attire.

When Apurba reached the lane by the side of the village pool, the same peal of laughter rang through the sky which he had heard the day before; and while he stood shamefaced and irresolute, looking about him, the culprit came out of her ambuscade and flung the patent leather shoes before him and tried to escape. Apurba rushed after her quickly and made her captive, holding her by the wrist. Mrinmayi writhed and wriggled, but could not set herself free. A sunbeam fell upon her mischievous face through a gap in the branches overhead, and Apurba gazed intently into her eyes, like a traveller peering through the limpid water of a rushing stream at the glistening pebbles below. He seemed to hesitate to complete his adventure, and slowly relaxed his hold and let his captive escape. If Apurba had boxed Mrinmayi's ears in anger, that would have seemed more natural to the girl than this silent incompleteness of punishment.

3

It is difficult to understand why a young man of culture and learning like Apurba should be so anxious to reveal his worth to this slip of a village girl. What harm would there be, if, in her pitiful ignorance, she should ignore him and choose that foolish poor Rakhal as her companion? Why should he struggle to prove to her that he wrote a monthly article in the journal *Visvadip*, and that a manuscript book of no mean size was waiting for publication in the bottom of his trunk, along with his scent bottles, tinted note-paper, harmonium lessons, etc.

In the evening Apurba's mother asked him: "Have you approved of your bride?"

Apurba said with a slight hesitation: "Yes, I like one of the girls."

"One of the girls!" she asked, "why, what do you mean?"

After a great deal of beating about the bush she found out that her son had selected Mrinmayi for his bride. When she grasped this fact she greatly lost her respect for the B.A. degree. Then followed a long struggle between them. At last the mother persuaded herself that Mrinmayi was not wholly impervious to improvement. She began to suspect also that the girl's face had a charm of its own, but the next moment the cropped head of hair came to her mind and gave her a feeling of disgust. Recognizing, however, "that hair is more amenable to reason than human nature, she felt consoled, and the betrothal was made.

Mrinmayi's father got the news. He was a clerk in an office at a small distant river station of a steamship company. He was engaged all day in selling tickets and loading and unloading cargo, living in a small hut with a corrugated iron roof. His eyes overflowed with tears when he got the letter telling him what had happened. How much was pleasure and how much was pain would be difficult to analyse.

Ishan applied to the head office in Calcutta for leave of absence. The reason of the betrothal seemed insufficient to the English manager of the company and the application was rejected. Ishan then asked for a postponement of the marriage till the autumn holidays; but he was told by the mother of the bridegroom that the most auspicious day for the marriage that year fell in the last week of the current month. So Ishan went on selling tickets and loading and unloading cargo with a heavy heart—his petitions rejected from both sides. After this, Mrinmayi's mother and all the matrons of the village began to admonish the girl about the future household duties. She was warned that love of play, quickness of movement, loudness of laughter, companionship of boys and disregard of good manners in eating would not be tolerated in her husband's house. They were completely successful in proving the terrible cramped constraint of married life. Mrinmayi took the proposal of her marriage as a sentence of life-imprisonment, with hanging at the end of it. Like an unmanageable little pony, she took the bit between her teeth and said, "I'm not going to be married."

4

But she had to marry after all. And then began her lesson. The whole universe shrank for her within the walls of her mother-in-law's household. The latter began at once her reformation duties. She hardened her face and said:

"My child, you are not a baby. The vulgar loudness of your behaviour won't suit our family."

The moral which Mrinmayi learnt from these words was that she must find some more suitable place for herself and she became invisible that very afternoon. They went on vainly searching for her till her friend Rakhal played the traitor, and revealed her hiding place in a deserted, broken down wooden chariot once used for taking out the image of the god for an airing. After this, the atmosphere of her mother-in-law's home became intolerably hot. Rain came down at night.

Apurba, coming close to Mrinmayi in his bed, whispered to her: "Mrinmayi, don't you love me?" Mrinmayi broke out: "No, I shall never love you!"

"But what harm have I done you?" said Apurba.

"Why did you marry me?" was the reply. To give a satisfactory explanation to this question was difficult, but Apurba said to himself: 'I must win, in the end, this rebellious heart.'

On the next day, the mother-in-law observed some signs of petulance in Mrinmayi and shut her up in a room. When Mrinmayi could find no way to get out, she tore the bed sheet to rags with her teeth in vain anger, and flinging herself on the floor burst out weeping and calling in agony: "Father, father!"

Just then somebody came and sat by her. He tried to arrange her dishevelled hair as she turned from side to side, but Mrinmayi angrily shook her head and pushed his hand away. Apurba (for it was he) bent his face to her ear and whispered:

"I have secretly opened the gate; let us run away by the back door."

Mrinmayi again violently shook her head and said: "No."

Apurba tried to raise her face gently by the chin saying: "Do look who is there." Rakhal had come and was standing foolishly by the door looking at Mrinmayi. But the girl pushed away Apurba's hand without raising her face.

He said "Rakhal has come to play with you. Won't you come?"

She said: "No!" Rakhal was greatly relieved to be allowed to run away from this scene.

Apurba sat still and silent. Mrinmayi wept and wept, till she was so tired that she fell asleep; then Apurba went out silently and shut the door.

The next day Mrinmayi received a letter from her father, in which he expressed his regret for not being able to be present at the marriage of his darling daughter. He ended with his blessings. The girl went to her mother-in-law and said: "I must go to my father."

A scolding began at once: "Your father! what a thing to ask. Your father has no decent house for himself—how can you go to him?"

Mrinmayi came back to her room in despair and cried to herself, "Father, take me away from this place! I have nobody here to love me. I shall die if I am left here."

In the depth of the night, when her husband fell asleep, she quietly opened the door and went out of the house. It was cloudy, yet the moonlight was strong enough to show her the path. But Mrinmayi had no idea which was the way to reach her father. She had a belief that the road, which the post runners took, led to all the addresses of all the men in the world.

So she went that way, and was quite tired out with walking when the night was nearly ended.

The early birds doubtfully twittered their greetings to the morning, when Mrinmayi came to the end of the road at the river-bank where there was a big bazaar. Just then she heard the clatter of the iron ring of the mail runner. She rushed to him and in her eager, tired voice cried: "I want to go to my father at Kushiganj. Do take me with you."

The postman told her hurriedly that he did not know where Kushiganj was and the next moment wakened up the boatman of the mail boat and sailed away. He had no time either to pity or to question.

By the time Mrinmayi had descended the landing stairs and called a boat, the street and the river-bank were fully awake. Before the boatman could answer, some one from a boat near at hand called out:

"Hallo, Mrinu! How on earth could you get here?"

The girl replied in all eagerness: "Banamali, I

must go to my father at Kushiganj. Please take me in your boat!"

This boatman belonged to her own village and knew all about the wild untameable girl. He said to her: "You want to go to your father? That's good. I'll take you."

Mrinmayi got into the boat. The clouds thickened and the rain came down in showers. The river, swollen by the monsoon, rocked the boat, and Mrinmayi fell asleep. When she woke up, she found herself in her own bed in her mother-in-law's house.

The maidservant began scolding her the moment she saw her awake. The mother-in-law came next. As she entered, Mrinmayi opened her eyes wide and silently looked in her face. But when the mother-in-law made a reference to the ill-breeding of Mrinmayi's family, the girl rushed out of her room and entered the next and shut the door from the inside.

Apurba came to his mother and said: "Mother, I don't see any harm in sending Mrinmayi for just a few days to her father's house."

The mother's reply was to scold Apurba in unmeasured terms for selecting this one girl from all the suitable brides who might have been had for the mere asking.

5

In the middle of the night, Apurba awakened Mrinmayi and said: "Mrinmayi, are you ready to go to your father?" She clutched his hand and said: "Yes."

Apurba whispered: "Then come. Let us run away from this place. I have got a boat ready at the landing. Come."

Mrinmayi cast a grateful glance at her husband's face, and got up and dressed, and was ready to go. Apurba left a letter for his mother, and then both of them left the house together hand in hand.

This was the first time that Mrinmayi had put her hand into her husband's with a spontaneous feeling of dependence. They went on their journey along the lonely village road through the depth of the night.

When they reached the landing stage, they got into a boat, and in spite of the turbulent joy which she felt Mrinmayi fell asleep. The next day—what emancipation, what unspeakable bliss it was! They passed by all the different villages, markets, cultivated fields, and groups of boats at anchor near some *ghāt*. Mrinmayi began to ply her husband with questions about every little trifle: where were those boats coming from, what were their cargoes, what was the name of that village?—questions whose answers were not in the text-books which Apurba studied in his college. His friends might be concerned to hear that Apurba's answers did not always tally with the truth. He would not hesitate for a moment to describe bags of sesame as linseed, and the village of Panchbere as Rainagar, or to point out the district magistrate's court as the landlord's office. Whatever answer she got, Mrinmayi was fully satisfied, never doubting its accuracy.

The next day the boat reached Kushiganj. Ishan, seated on his office stool, in his hut dimly lighted with a square oil-lantern, was deep in his accounts before his small desk, his big ledger open before him, when this young pair entered the room. Mrinmayi at once called out:

"Father!"

Such a word, uttered in so sweet a voice, had never sounded before in that corrugated iron room. Ishan could hardly restrain his tears and sat dumb for a moment, vainly seeking for some greeting. He was in great confusion how fitly to receive the young married couple in his office, crowded with bales of jute and piled up ledgers, which had also to serve him for a bedroom. And then about the meals—the poor man had to cook for himself his own simple dinner, but how could he offer that to his guests? Mrinmayi said, "Father, let us cook the food ourselves."

And Apurba joined in this proposal with great zest. In this room, with all its lack of space for man and food, their joy welled up in full abundance, like the jet of water thrown up all the higher because the opening of the fountain is narrow.

Three days were passed in this manner. Steamers came to stop at the landing stage all day long with their noisy crowd of men. At last, in the evening, the river-bank would become deserted and then—what freedom! And the cooking preparations in which the art of cookery was not carried to its perfection—what fun it was! And the jokes and mock quarrels about the mock deficiencies in Mrinmayi's domestic skill—what absurd carryings on! But it had to come to an end at last. Apurba did not dare to prolong his French leave, and Ishan also thought it was wise for them to return.

When the culprits reached home, the mother remained sulkily silent. She never even blamed them for what they had done so as to give them an opportunity to explain their conduct. This sullen silence became at last intolerable, and Apurba expressed his intention of going back to college in order to study Law. The mother, affecting indifference, said to him: "What about your wife?"

Apurba answered: "Let her remain here."

"Oh, no, no!" cried the mother, "you should take her with you."

Apurba said in a voice of annoyance: "Very well."

The preparation went on for their departure to the town, and on the night before leaving Apurba, coming to his bed, found Mrinmayi in tears. This hurt him greatly and he cried:

Mrinmayi, don't you want to come to Calcutta with me?"

The girl replied: "No!"

Apurba's next question was, "Don't you love me?" But the question remained unanswered. There are times when answers to such questions are absolutely simple, but at other times they become too complex for a young girl to answer.

Apurba asked : "Do you feel unwilling to leave Rakhal behind?"

Mrinmayi instantly answered: "Yes". For a moment this young man, who was proud of his B.A. degree, felt a needle prick of jealousy deep down in his heart, and said:

"I shan't be able to come back home for a long time." Mrinmayi had nothing to say. "It may be two years or more," he added. Mrinmayi told him with coolness, "You had better bring back with you, for Rakhal, a Roger's knife with three blades."

Apurba sat up and asked:

"Then you mean to stay on here?"

Mrinmayi said:

"Yes, I shall go to my own mother."

Apurba breathed a deep sigh and said:

"Very well: I shall not come home, until you write me a letter asking me to come to you. Are you very, very glad?"

Mrinmayi thought this question needed no answer, and fell asleep. Apurba got no sleep that night.

When it was nearly dawn, Apurba awakened Mrinmayi and said:

"Mrinu, it is time to go. Let me take you to your mother's house."

When his wife got up from her bed, Apurba held her by both hands and said:

"I have a prayer to make to you. I have helped you several times and I want to claim my reward."

Mrinmayi was surprised and said:

"What?"

Apurba answered:

"Mrinu, give me a kiss out of pure love."

When the girl heard this absurd request and saw Apurba's solemn face, she burst out laughing. When it was over, she held her face for a kiss, but broke out laughing again. After a few more attempts, she gave it up. Apurba pulled her ear gently as a mild punishment.

7

When Mrinmayi came to her mother's house, she was surprised to find that it was not as pleasant to her as before. Time seemed to hang heavily on her hands, and she wondered in her mind what was lacking in the familiar home surroundings. Suddenly it seemed to her that the whole house and village were deserted and she longed to go to Calcutta. She did not know that even on that last night the earlier portion of her life, to which she clung, had changed its aspect before she knew it. Now she could easily shake off her past associations as the tree sheds its dead leaves. She did not understand that her destiny had struck the blow and severed her youth from her childhood, with its magic blade, in such a subtle manner that they kept together even after the stroke; but directly she moved, one half of her life fell from the other and Mrinmayi looked at it in wonder. The young girl, who used to occupy the old bedroom in this house, no longer existed; all her memory hovered round another bed in another bedroom.

Mrinmayi refused to go out of doors any longer, and her laughter had a strangely different ring. Rakhal became slightly afraid of her. He gave up all thought of playing with her.

One day, Mrinmayi came to her mother and asked her:

"Mother, please take me to my mother-in-law's house."

After this, one morning the mother-in-law was surprised to see Mrinmayi come and touch the ground with her forehead before her feet. She got up at once and took her in her arms. Their union was complete in a moment, and the cloud of misunderstanding was swept away leaving the atmosphere glistening with the radiance of tears.

When Mrinmayi's body and mind became filled with womanhood, deep and tender, it gave her an aching pain. Her eyes became sad, like the shadow of rain upon some lake, and she put these questions to her husband in her own mind—'Why did you not have the patience to understand me, when I was late in understanding you? Why did you put up with my disobedience, when I refused to follow you to Calcutta?'

Suddenly she came to fathom the look in Apurba's eyes when, on that morning, he had caught hold of her hand by the village pool and then slowly released her. She remembered, too, the futile flights of that kiss, which had never reached its goal, and was now like a thirsty bird haunting that past opportunity. She recollected how Apurba had said to her that he would never come back until he had received from her a message asking him to do so; and she sat down at once to write a letter. The gilt-edged notepaper which Apurba had given her was brought out of its box, and with great care she began to write in a big hand, smudging her fingers with ink. With her first word she plunged into the subject without addressing him:

Why don't you write to me? How are you? And please come home.

She could think of no other words to say. But though the important message had been given, yet unfortunately the unimportant words occupy the greatest space in human communication. She racked her brains to add a few more words to what she had written, and then wrote:

This time don't forget to write me letters and write how you are, and come back home, and mother is quite well. Our black cow had a calf last night—

Here she came to the end of her resources. She put her letter into the envelope and poured out all her love as she wrote the name: Srijukta Babu Apurbakrishna Roy. She did not know that anything more was needed by way of an address, so the letter did not reach its goal, and the postal authorities were not to blame for it.

It was vacation time. Yet Apurba never came home. The mother thought that he was nourishing anger against her. Mrinmayi was certain that her letter was not well enough written to satisfy him. At last the mother said to her daughter-in-law, "Apurba has been absent for so long that I am thinking of going to Calcutta to see him. Would you like to come with me?"

Mrinmayi gave a violent nod of assent. Then she ran to her room and shut herself in. She fell upon her bed, clutched the pillow to her breast, and gave vent to her feelings by laughing and excited movements. When this fit was over, she became grave and sad and sat up on the bed and wept in silence.

Without telling Apurba, these two repentant women went to Calcutta to ask for Apurba's forgiveness. The mother had a son-in-law in Calcutta, and so she put up at his house. That very same evening, Apurba broke his promise and began to write a letter to Mrinmayi. But he found no terms of endearment fit to express his love, and felt disgusted with his mother tongue for its poverty. But when he got a letter from his brother-in-law, informing him of the arrival of his mother and inviting him to dinner, he hastened to his sister's house without delay.

The first question he asked his mother, when he met her, was: "Mother, is everybody at home quite well?"

The mother answered: "Yes, I have come here to take you back home."

Apurba said that he thought it was not necessary on her part to have taken all this trouble for such a purpose, and he had his examination before him, etc., etc.

At dinner his sister asked him why he had not brought his wife with him when he returned to Calcutta this time. Apurba began to say very solemnly that he had his law examination to think of, etc., etc.

The brother-in-law cut in smiling:

"All this is a mere excuse: the real reason is that he is afraid of us."

His sister replied: "You are indeed a terrifying person! The poor child may well get a shock when she sees you."

Thus the laughter and jokes became plentiful, but Apurba remained silent. He was accusing his mother in his mind for not having had the consideration to bring Mrinmayi with her. Then he thought that possibly his mother had tried, but failed, owing to Mrinmayi's unwillingness, and he felt afraid even to question his mother about it; the whole scheme of things seemed to him full of incorrigible blunders.

When the dinner was over, it came on to rain and his sister said, "*Dada,* you sleep here."

But Apurba replied, "No, I must go home. I have work to do."

The brother-in-law said, "How absurd! You have no one at home to call you to account for your absence, and you needn't be anxious."

Then his sister told him that he was looking very tired, and it was better for him to leave the company and go to bed. Apurba went to his bedroom and found it in darkness. His sister asked him if he wanted a light, but he said that he preferred the dark. When his sister had left, he groped his way to the bedstead and prepared to get into bed.

All of a sudden a tender pair of arms, with a jingle of bracelets, were flung round his neck, and two lips soft as flower petals almost smothered him with kisses wet with tears.

At first it startled Apurba greatly, but then he came to know that those kisses, which had been obstructed once by laughter, had now found their completion in tears.

The Parrots Training

Once upon a time there was a bird. It was ignorant. It sang all right, but never recited scriptures. It hopped pretty frequently, but lacked manners.

Said the Raja to himself: 'Ignorance is costly in the long run. For fools consume as much food as their betters, and yet give nothing in return.'

He called his nephews to his presence and told them that the bird must have a sound schooling.

The pundits were summoned, and at once went to the root of the matter. They decided that the ignorance of birds was due to their natural habit of living in poor nests. Therefore, according to the pundits, the first thing necessary for this bird's education was a suitable cage.

The pundits had their rewards and went home happy.

A golden cage was built with gorgeous decorations. Crowds came to see it from all parts of the world.

"Culture, captured and caged!" exclaimed some, in a rapture of ecstasy, and burst into tears.

Others remarked: "Even if culture be missesd, the cage will remain, to the end, a substantial fact. How fortunate for the bird!"

The goldsmith filled his bag with money and lost no time in sailing homewards.

The pundit sat down to educate the bird. With proper deliberation he took his pinch of snuff, as he said: "Text-books can never be too many for our purpose!"

The nephews brought together an enormous crowd of scribes. They copied from books, and copied from copies, till the manuscripts were piled up to an unreachable height.

Men murmured in amazement: "Oh, the tower of culture, egregiously high! The end of it lost in the clouds!"

The scribes, with light hearts, hurried home, their pockets heavily laden.

The nephews were furiously busy keeping the cage in proper trim.

As their constant scrubbing and polishing went on, the people said with satisfaction: "This is progress indeed!"

Men were employed in large numbers, and supervisors were still more numerous. These, with their cousins of all different degrees of distance, built a palace for themselves and lived there happily ever after.

Whatever may be its other deficiencies, the world is never in want of fault-finders; and they went about saying that every creature remotely connected with the cage flourished beyond words, excepting only the bird.

When this remark reached the Raja's ears, he summoned his nephews before him and said: "My dear nephews, what is this that we hear?"

The nephews said in answer: "Sire, let the testimony of the goldsmiths and the pundits, the scribes and the supervisors, be taken, if the truth is to be known food is scarce with the fault-finders, and that is why their tongues have gained in sharpness."

The explanation was so luminously satisfactory that the Raja decorated each one of his nephews with his own rare jewels.

The Raja at length, being desirous of seeing with his own eyes how his Education Department busied itself with the little bird, made his appearance one day at the great Hall of Learning.

From the gate rose the sounds of conch-shells and gongs, horns, bugles and trumpets, cymbals, drums and kettle-drums, tomtoms, tambourines, flutes, fifes, barrel-organs and bagpipes. The pundits began chanting *mantras* with their topmost voices, while the goldsmiths, scribes, supervisors, and their numberless cousins of all different degrees of distance, loudly raised a round of cheers.

The nephews smiled and said: "Sire, what do you think of it all?"

The Raja said: "It does seem so fearfully like a sound principle of Education!"

Mightily pleased, the Raja was about to remount his elephant, when the fault-finder, from behind some bush, cried out: "Maharaja, have you seen the bird?"

"Indeed, I have not!" exclaimed the Raja, "I completely forgot about the bird."

Turning back, he asked the pundits about the method they followed in instructing the bird.

It was shown to him. He was immensely impressed. The method was so stupendous that the bird looked ridiculously unimportant in comparison. The Raja was satisfied that there was no flaw in the arrangements. As for any complaint from the bird itself, that simply could not be expected. Its throat was so completely choked with the leaves from the books that it could neither whistle nor whisper. It sent a thrill through one's body to watch the process.

This time, while remounting his elephant, the Raja ordered his State Earpuller to give a thorough good pull at both the ears of the fault-finder.

The bird thus crawled on, duly and properly, to the safest verge of inanity. In fact, its progress was satisfactory in the extreme. Nevertheless, nature occasionally triumphed over training, and when the morning light peeped into the bird's cage it sometimes fluttered its wings in a reprehensible manner. And, though it is hard to believe, it pitifully pecked at its bars with its feeble beak.

"What impertinence!" growled the *kotwal*.

The blacksmith, with his forge and hammer, took his place in the Raja's Department of Education. Oh, what resounding blows! The iron chain was soon completed, and the bird's wings were clipped.

The Raja's brothers-in-law looked black, and shook their heads, saying: "These birds not only lack good sense, but also gratitude!"

With text-book in one hand and baton in the other, the pundits gave the poor bird what may fitly be called lessons!

The *kotwal* was honoured with a title for his watchfulness and the blacksmith for his skill in forging chains.

The bird died.

Nobody had the least notion how long ago this had happened. The fault-finder was the first man to spread the rumour.

The Raja called his nephews and asked them: "My dear nephews, what is this that we hear?"

The nephews said: "Sire, the bird's education has been completed."

"Does it hop?" the Raja enquired.

"Never!" said the nephews.

"Does it fly?"

"No."

"Bring me the bird," said the Raja.

The bird was brought to him, guarded by the *kotwal* and the sepoys and the sowars. The Raja poked its body with his finger. Only its inner stuffing of book-leaves rustled.

Outside the window, the murmur of the spring breeze amongst the newly budded *asoka* leaves made the April morning wistful.

The Trial of the Horse

Brahma, the creator, was very near the end of his task of creation when a new idea struck him.

He sent for the Store-keeper and said: "O keeper of the stores, bring to my factory a quantity of each of the five elements. For I am ready to create another creature."

"Lord of the universe," the Store-keeper replied, "when in the first flush of creative extravagance you began to turn out such exaggerations as elephants and whales and pythons and tigers, you took no count of the stock. Now, all the elements that have density and force are nearly used up. The supply of earth and water and fire has become inconveniently scanty, while of air and ether there is as much as is good for us and a good deal more."

The four-headed deity looked perplexed and pulled at his four pairs of moustaches. At last he said: "The limitedness of material gives all the more scope to originality. Send me whatever you have left."

This time Brahma was excessively sparing with the earth, water and fire. The new creature was not given either horns or claws, and his teeth were only meant for chewing, not for biting. The prudent care with which fire was used in his formation made him necessary in war without making him warlike.

This animal was the Horse.

The reckless expenditure of air and ether, which went into his composition, was amazing. And, in consequence, he perpetually struggled to outreach the wind, to outrun space itself. The other animals run only when they have a reason, but the horse would run for nothing whatever, as if to run out of his own skin. He had no desire to chase, or to kill, but only to fly on and on till he dwindled into a dot, melted into a swoon, blurred into a shadow, and vanished into vacancy.

The Creator was glad. He had given for his other creatures habitations—to some the forests, to other the caves. But in his enjoyment of the disinterested spirit of speed in the Horse, he gave him an open meadow under the very eye of heaven.

By the side of this meadow lived Man.

Man has his delight in pillaging and piling things up. And he is never happy till these grow into a burden. So, when he saw this new creature pursuing the wind and kicking at the sky, he said to himself: "If only I can bind and secure this Horse, I can use his broad back for carrying my loads."

So one day he caught the Horse.

Then Man put a saddle on the Horse's back and a spiky bit in his mouth. He regularly had hard rubbing and scrubbing to keep him fit, and there were the whip and spurs to remind him that it was wrong to have his own will.

Man also put high walls round the Horse, lest if left at large in the open the creature might escape him.

So it came to pass, that while the Tiger who had his forest remained in the forest, the Lion who had his cave remained in the cave, the Horse who once had his open meadow came to spend his days in a stable. Air and ether had roused in the horse longings for deliverance, but they swiftly delivered him into bondage.

When he felt that bondage did not suit him, the Horse kicked at the stable walls.

But this hurt his hoofs much more than it hurt the wall. Still some of the plaster came off and the wall lost its beauty.

Man felt aggrieved.

"What ingratitude!" he cried. "Do I not give him food and drink? Do I not keep highly-paid men-servants to watch over him day and night? Indeed he is hard to please."

In their desperate attempts to please the Horse, the men-servants fell upon him and so vigorously applied all their winning methods that he lost his power to kick and a great deal more besides.

Then Man called his friends and neighbours together, and said to them exultingly: "Friends, did you ever see so devoted a steed as mine?"

"Never!" they replied. "He seems as still as ditch water and as mild as the religion you profess."

The Horse, as is well known, had no horns, no claws, nor adequate teeth, at his birth. And, when on the top of this, all kicking at the walls and even into emptiness had been stopped, the only way to give vent to his feelings was to neigh.

But that disturbed Man's sleep.

Moreover, this neighing was not likely to impress the neighbours as a paean of devotion and thankfulness. So Man invented devices to shut the Horse's mouth.

But the voice cannot be altogether suppressed so long as the mistake is made of leaving any breath in the body. Therefore a spasmodic sound of moaning came from his throat now and then.

One day this noise reached Brahma's ears.

The Creator woke up from his meditation. It gave him a start when he glanced at the meadow and saw no sign of the Horse.

"This is all your doing," cried Brahma, in anger to Yama, the god of death: "You have taken away the Horse !"

"Lord of all creatures!" Death replied: "All your worst suspicions you keep only for me. But most of the calamities in your beautiful world will be explained if you turn your eyes in the direction of Man."

Brahma looked below. He saw a small enclosure, walled in, from which the dolorous moaning of his Horse came fitfully.

Brahma frowned in anger.

"Unless you set free my Horse," said he: "I shall take care that he grows teeth and claws like the Tiger."

"That would be ungodly," cried man: "to encourage ferocity. All the same, if I may speak plain truth about a creature of your own make, this Horse is not fit to be set free. It was for his eternal good that I built him this stable——this marvel of architecture."

Brahma remained obdurate.

"I bow to your wisdom," said Man: "but if, after seven days, you still think that your meadow is better for him than my stable, I will humbly own defeat."

After this Man set to work.

He made the Horse go free, but hobbled his front legs. The result was so vastly diverting that it was enough to make even a frog burst his sides with laughter.

Brahma, from the height of his heaven, could see the comic gait of his Horse, but not the tragic rope which hobbled him. He was mortified to find his own creature openly exposing its divine maker to ridicule.

"It was an absurd blunder of mine", he cried, "closely touching the sublime."

"Grandsire," said Man with a pathetic show of sympathy, "what can I do for this unfortunate creature? If there is a meadow in your heaven, I am willing to take trouble to transport him thither."

"Take him back to your stable!" cried Brahma in dismay.

"Merciful God!" cried Man, "what a great burden it will be for mankind!"

"It is the burden of humanity," muttered Brahma.

Old Man's Ghost

At the time of the Old Man Leader's death, the entire population wailed, "What will be our lot when you go?"

Hearing this, the Old Man himself felt sad. 'Who indeed,' thought he, 'will keep these people quiescent when I have gone?'

Death cannot be evaded, however. Yet the gods took pity and said: "Why worry? Let this fellow go on sitting on their shoulders even as a ghost. Man dies but a ghost does not."

The people of the country were greatly relieved.

For, worries come if only you believe in a future. Believing in ghosts you are freed from burden, all the worries enter the ghost's head. Yet the ghost has no head, so it does not suffer from headaches either, not for anybody's sake.

Those, who out of sheer wrong habit still attempt to think for themselves, get their ears boxed by the ghost. From this ghostly boxing you can neither free yourself nor can you escape it; against it is neither appeal nor any judgement at all.

The entire population, ghost-ridden, now walks with eyes shut. "The most ancient form of movement, this, with eyes shut," the philosophers assure them, "moving like blind fate, we call it. Thus moved the first eyeless amoeba. In the grass, in the trees, this habit of movement is still customary."

Hearing which, the ghost-ridden land feels its own primitive aristocracy. And it is greatly delighted.

The Ghost's *nayeb* is the inspector of the prison. The walls of the prison-house are not visible to the eye. And so it is impossible to imagine how to pierce those walls and get free.

In the prison-house one has to slave at turning the oil-press night and day but not even an ounce of oil is produced which is marketable; only the energy of men goes out in extracting the oil. When their energy goes out, men become exceedingly peaceful. And thus in that ghost's realm whatever else there might not be— food, or clothing or health—tranquillity remains.

How great is the tranquillity is proved by one example: in other lands excessive ghostly tyranny makes men restless and seek for a medicine-man. Here such a thought cannot arise. For the medicine-man himself has already been possessed by the ghost.

Thus the days would have passed; nobody would have questioned the ghostly administration. Forever they could have taken pride that their future, like a pet lamb, was tied to the ghost's peg; such a creature neither bleated nor baa'd, it sprawled dumb on the dust, useless as dust.

Only, for a slight reason, some little trouble arose. It was that the other countries of the world were not ghost-ridden. Their oil-presses turned so that the extracted oil might be used for keeping the wheels of men's chariots moving forward, not for crushing the heart and pouring heart's blood into the paws of the ghost. So, men there have not yet been completely pacified. They were terribly wakeful.

All over the ghostly empire:

the baby sleeps; quiet is the neighbourhood.

That is comforting for the baby, and for the baby's guardian too; as to the neighbourhood, we have already seen how it is.

But there is the other line,

the invaders enter the land.

Thus the rhythm is completed—otherwise for lack of one foot, this history would have been crippled.

The pedants and pundits are asked: "Why is it thus?"

They toss their heads together and say: "Not the ghost's fault this, nor of the ghost-ridden land: the fault lies with the invader. Why does the invader come?"

"How right!" they all admit. And everyone feels exceedingly comforted.

Whosoever the fault might be, near the back-door of the house loiter the ghost's emissaries, and in the open street outside everywhere roam the non-ghost's emissaries; the householder can hardly stay in his house, to stir out of doors is also impossible. From one side they shout "pay the taxes?" and from the other also they shout "pay the taxes!"

Now the problem is, "how to pay the taxes?"

Up to now, from north, south, east and west, *bulbulis* of all species have come in large flocks, and gorged themselves with the corn, nobody was mindful. With all those who are mindful, these people avoid contact, lest they have to do *prāyashchitta* for contamination. But those other folk who are mindful have a way of coming suddenly very near to them indeed and they do not observe any penance either.

The pedants and pundits open the text and say: "Pure are the unmindful, and impure the mindful ones; so be indifferent to these latter. Remember the sacred words, 'awake are those who sleepeth.'"

And hearing this the people are hugely delighted.

But, in spite of this, the query cannot be stopped, "how to pay the taxes?"

From the burning-ground, from the burial-ground the wild winds bring the loud answer: "Pay the taxes with the price of your modesty, with your honour, with your conscience, with your heart's blood."

The trouble with questions is: when they come they do not come singly. So, another question has arisen: "Will the ghostly reign itself remain for ever?"

Hearing this, all the lullaby-singing aunts and uncles put their hands on their ears in horror and exclaim: "Perdition! Never in our fathers' life have we heard of such a thing! What will then have happened to our sleep, the most ancient sleep, the sleep which is earlier than all awakening?"

"That I see", the questioner persists: "but these most modern flocks of *bulbulis* and these very much present invaders—what about *them*?"

"To the *bulbulis* we shall repeat the name of Krishna," assert the aunts and uncles, "and so shall we do to the invaders."

The ignorant youths get impertinent and bluster out; "Drive the ghost out we shall—whatever the means."

The ghost's *nayeb* rolls his eyes in anger and shouts, "Shut up! The oil-press hasn't stopped grinding. No, not yet."

Hearing which the baby of the land falls silent, and then turns to sleep.

The great fact is, the Old Man is neither alive nor dead, but is a ghost. He neither stirs the country up nor ever relaxes his grip.

Inside the country, one or two men—those who never utter a word in daytime for fear of the *nayeb*—join their palms together and implore: "Old Man Leader, is it not yet time for you to leave us?"

"You fool," answers the Old Man, "I neither hold, nor let go; if you leave, then I have also left."

"But we are afraid, Old Man Leader!"

"That is where the ghost enters,"—comes the answer.

Great News

Said Kusmi "You would give me all the big news—so you promised, didn't you, *Dādāmashāy* How else could I get educated?"

Answered *Dādāmashāy:* "But such a sack of big news there would be to carry—with so much of rubbish in it."

"Why not leave those out?"

"Little else would remain, then. And that remainder you will think as small news. But that would be the real news."

"Give it to me—the real news."

"So I will."

"Well, *Dādāmashāy* let me see what skill you have. Tell me the great news of these days, making it ever so small."

"Listen."

Work was proceeding in peace.

In a *mahājani* boat there started a row between the sail and the oars.

The oars came clattering to the court of the Boatman, and said: "This cannot be endured any longer. That braggart sail of yours, swelling himself, calls us *chhoto lok*. Because we, tied night and day to the lower planks, must toil, pushing the waters as we proceed, while he moves by whim, not caring for the push of any one's hand. And so he is a *bara lok*. You must decide who is more worthy. If we are *chhoto lok* the inferior ones, we shall resign in a body. Let us see how you make your boat move."

The Boatman, seeing danger ahead, called the oars aside and whispered secretly: "Do not give ear to his words, brothers. He speaks an empty language, that sail. If you strong fellows did not work away, staking life and death, the boat would lie inert altogether. And that sail—he sits there in hallow luxury, perched on the top. At the slightest touch of stormy wind he flops, folds himself up, and lies low on the boat's thatch. Then all his vain flutterings are silenced, not a word from him at all. But in weal and woe, in danger and in crisis, on the way to the market and the ghat, you are my constant support. It is a pity that you have to carry that useless burden of luxury, to and fro. Who says you are *chhoto lok?*"

But the Boatman was afraid, lest these words be overheard by the sail. So he came to him and whispered into his ear: "Mr. Sail, none ever can be compared with you. Who says that you drive the boat, that is the work of labourers. You move at your own pleasure, and your pals and comrades follow you at your slightest gesture and bidding. And whenever you feel out of breath, you would flop down easefully, and rest. Do not lend your ear, friend, to the parleying of those low-bred oars; so firmly have I tied them up, that splutter as they might, they cannot but work as slaves."

Hearing this, the sail stretched himself, and yawned mightily.

But the signs were not good. Those oars are hard-boned fellows, now they lie aslant but who knows when they will stand up straight, slap at the sail and shatter his pride into shreds. Then the world would know that it is the oars who make the boat move, come storm come tornado, whether it be upstream or at ebb-tide.

Queried Kusmi: "Your big news, is it so small as this? You are joking."

Said *Dādāmashāy*: "Joking it seems to be. Very soon this news will become big indeed."

"And then?"

"Then your *Dādāmashāy* will practise keeping time with the strokes of those oars."

"And I?"

"Where the oars creak too muck, you will pour a drop of oil."

Dādāmashāy continued: "True news appears small, like the seeds. And then comes the tree with its branches and foliage. Do you understand now?"

"So I do," said Kusmi. Her face showed that she had not understood. But Kusmi had one virture, she would not easily admit it to her *Dādāmashāy* that she would not understand. That she is less clever than *Iru Māshi* is better kept concealed.